William Falconer

Dissertation on St. Paul's Voyage from Caesarea to Puteoli

and on the Apostle's shipwreck on the Island Melite

William Falconer

Dissertation on St. Paul's Voyage from Caesarea to Puteoli
and on the Apostle's shipwreck on the Island Melite

ISBN/EAN: 9783337410056

Printed in Europe, USA, Canada, Australia, Japan

Cover: Foto ©Andreas Hilbeck / pixelio.de

More available books at **www.hansebooks.com**

DISSERTATION

ON

ST. PAUL'S VOYAGE

FROM

CÆSAREA TO PUTEOLI;

AND ON

THE APOSTLE'S SHIPWRECK ON THE ISLAND MELITE.

BY

WILLIAM FALCONER, M.D., F.R.S.

Third Edition,

WITH ADDITIONAL NOTES BY

THOMAS FALCONER, Esq.,
(One of the Judges of County Courts.)

~~~~~~~~~

Οὕτως ἀταλαίπωρος τοῖς πολλοῖς ἡ ζήτησις τῆς ἀληθείας, καὶ ἐπὶ τα ἑτοίμα μᾶλλον τρέπονται.—*Thucydides*, i. 20.

" So indifferent to the multitude is the search after truth that they prefer to take up with what is ready at hand."

" The highest ethical law of science is the love of truth, the conscientious search for truth, even when it is opposed to the opinions we have learned to cherish."

~~~~~~~~~

LONDON:

WILLIAMS AND NORGATE,

14, HENRIETTA STREET, COVENT GARDEN,

AND 20, SOUTH FREDERICK STREET, EDINBURGH.

1872.

[The First Edition was published in 1817.]

IN this Third Edition a continuous form is given to the arguments which in the Second Edition were largely contained in notes imperfectly connected. This is done for the convenience of the reader and it will aid in making the object of this publication clear. The additions of T. F. are placed within brackets marked with these initials and some arguments taken from Mr. Bryant's work are marked B.

The authorities cited are given very much *in extenso*, in order to enable the reader to form his own conclusions correctly and to estimate the value of those expressed by former writers on the Shipwreck.

T. F

ERRATA, &c.

Page 40, line 20, for "Gosselin," read "Gossellin."

„ 44, line 1, for "Ambarcio," read "Ambracio."

„ 51, line 11, for "Italy," read "SICILY."

„ 55, line 8, after the word "alive" add "about."

„ 76, line 22, for "prow of" read "prow by."

„ 98, line 12 from bottom, for "stadiæ," read "stadia."

" *Tullius et Cicero Tironi suo* S. P. D. [Epist. ad Familiares, lib. xvi. Epist. 9]. Nos a te, ut scis, discessimus a. d. IV. Non. Novembr. [*Nov.* 2]. —Leucadem [*Santa Maura*] venimus a. d. VIII. Idus Novembr. [*Nov.* 6], a. d. VII. [*Nov.* 7] Actium: ibi propter tempestatem a. d. VI. Idus [*Nov.* 8] morati sumus. Inde a. d. V. Idus [*Nov.* 9] Corcyram [*Corfu*] bellissime navigavimus. Corcyræ fuimus usque a. d. XVI. Kalend. Decembr. [*Nov.* 16] tempestatibus retenti. — A. d. XV. Kalend. Decembr. [*Nov.* 17] a portu Corcyræorum ad Cassiopen [*Cape St. Catherine, Corfu*] stadia cxx processimus. Ibi retenti ventis sumus usque a. d. IX. Kalendas [*Nov.* 23]. Interea, qui cupide profecti sunt, multi naufragia fecerunt. Nos eo die cenati solvimus. Inde Austro [S.] lenissimo, cœlo sereno, nocte illa et die postero in Italiam ad Hydruntum [*Otranto*] ludibundi pervenimus eodemque vento postridie—id erat a. d. VII. Kalend. Decembr. [*Nov.* 25]—hora quarta Brundusium [*Brindisi*] venimus."

Cicero continued his voyage, and sailed to Otranto. If he had been at Malta, and not at Cassiope, the south wind which carried the ship from Corfu to Otranto could, in an equal space of time, have carried it from Malta to Syracuse. A voyage at the end of November or in the winter from Meleda to Syracuse was dangerous.

Cæsar, writing on the departure of Octavius from the Illyrian coast, called the people of Dalmatia "*barbari*"—"Sed post discessum Liburnarum ex Illyricis M. Octavius cum iis, quas habebat, navibus Salonas [*Spalato*] pervenit: ibique concitatis Dalmatis, *reliquisque barbaris*, Isam [*Lissa*] a Cæsaris amicitia avertit."—*De Bello Civili*, lib. iii. ch. 9.

USK, MONMOUTHSHIRE,
October 1, 1872.

DISSERTATION

ON

ST. PAUL'S VOYAGE.[a]

S T. PAUL having been accused before Festus, the Roman Acts xxv. 7.
Governor of Judæa, by the Jews, of divers crimes, availed
himself of his privilege, as a Roman citizen, of appealing unto
the Emperor in person, or of claiming to have his cause heard Ver. 11.
and adjudged before the imperial tribunal at Rome. In consequence of this claim being admitted, it became necessary
that he should be sent to that city; and he was accordingly, Ver. 12.
together with several other prisoners, delivered in charge to
Julius, a centurion of Augustus's band, in order that Julius Acts xxvii. 1.
might convey them to Rome.

The centurion so entrusted put his prisoners, and accompanied A.D. 60.
them himself, on board a ship of Adramyttium,[b] then lying at

---

[a] The present work was originally designed to accompany a new edition of
some of the tracts in the 'Geographi Minores,' and consisted of twenty-four
pages.

The third edition of the work of James Smith, Esq., of Jordan Hill, entitled
The Voyage and Shipwreck of St. Paul, 1866, is referred to in the additions
to this essay.

Philippi Cluveri, Sicilia Antiqua cum minoribus Insulis ei adjacentibus,
Lug. Bat. ex officina Elsiviriana, fol. 1619, p. 425. This book is useful for
its citations from the works of early writers; otherwise it gives no assistance.

Dissertations on the Wind Euroclydon and on the Island Melite, printed in
a work entitled 'A New System, or an Analysis of Antient Mythology,' by
Jacob Bryant, Esq., 3rd edition, vol. v. 8vo, 1807.

Georgius Ignatius: *D. Paulus Apostolus* in mari quod nunc Venetus Sinus
dicitur naufragus et Melitæ Dalmatensis insulæ post naufragium hospes.
4to, Venet. 1730.

Bochart, Samuel, of Rouen, born 1599, died 1667: *Opera*, 3 vol. folio.
Lug. Bat. 1712. *Geographia Sacra*, vol. i. ch. 26. His argument on the
Voyage is fully cited by Bryant.

[b] Adramyttium nearly retains its ancient name, being still called Adramyti.
It is situate in a small gulf that bears the same appellation, opposite the
island of Lesbos, in nearly 39° 35′ N. lat. and 27° 2′ E. long.

[Thessalonica, the Roman capital of Macedonia, at the head of the Thermaic

65

B

Cæsarea,[c] and, as we may infer, preparing to return homewards. It appears that they who conducted the ship meant to sail on their return by the coast of Asia. Accordingly, the next day, after they set sail, they touched at Sidon,[d] a noted city on the coast of Cœlesyria, lying in 33° 34′ N. lat., 35° 21′ E. long., and about a degree to the north of Cæsarea,[e] with some little deviation to the east. Here it seems they stayed some days; but how long we are not informed. On their loosing from Sidon, they found that their intentions of continuing their voyage along the coast of Asia Minor would be frustrated by contrary winds, which obliged them to pursue their voyage[f] under or on the southern side of the island of Cyprus, instead of the northern, as, according to their plan of sailing along the coast, they had at first proposed.[g]

Ver. 2.

Ver. 3.

Ver. 4.

Ver. 4.

Gulf, is nearly on the same latitude, being 40° 38′ 47″ N. lat. and 22° 57′ 22″ E. long. It was the chief station on the *Via Egnatia* between the Adriatic and the Hellespont. Its distance from Amphipolis (Acts xvii. 1) is sixty-seven miles. The western termination on the Adriatic of the Via Egnatia was Dyrrachium, and the common passage-port on the other side of that sea was Brundusium.—T. F.]

[e] Mr. Bryant thinks, but without foundation, that they set out from Ptolemais (Acre). The foregoing chapter ends with what was transacted at Cæsarea, and no account whatever is given of their journey to Ptolemais. They might have reached Sidon in one day from Cæsarea, as well as from Ptolemais.

[d] [The anchorage at Sidon is very much exposed to all winds that have westing, and there is generally a swell, which makes riding bad outside for large ships. Sidon is built on a hill close to the sea. The country about is beautifully cultivated. — *Sailing Directions*, p. 522, by Findlay, 1868. T. F.]

[e] Cæsarea is five miles to the southward of Tantûra anciently Dora. It was once the principal seaport of Samaria, and is now only to be distinguished by the ruins that surround it.

[See note on Cæsarea by the Rev. Dr. Traill (Translation of Josephus, p. liv. ed. 1868). "Almost engulphed in the sea, and half entombed by sand, nothing but the unstoried remains of barbarous times now rescue the site of splendid Cæsarea from utter obliteration. In advancing from this spot towards Carmel I noticed many not-to-be-mistaken evidences of the existence in former days of a great population; the face of the limestone rock, which for the most part walls-in the shore, is hewn into innumerable tombs."—*Mr. Tipping*, 1842. T. F.]

[f] ὑπεπλεύσαμεν.—Acts xxvii. 4. ὑποπλέω, *to sail under.*

[g] [The island of Cyprus is called by the Turks Kupris, and is situated between the latitudes of 34° 32′ and 35° 41′ north, and longitudes 32° 16′ and 34° 38′ east: it lies in an E. by N. and a W. by S. direction, being 41

The word referred to, literally translated, implies that they sailed *under* Cyprus, the North point being accounted to be uppermost[h] in ancient as well as in modern geography.[i]

Their course, after doubling the western point of the Isle of

---

leagues in length, and 11 in breadth. The rainy seasons are March, April, November, December, and January; in the winter, a sort of tornado, attended with hail, is not unfrequent. The most prevailing winds are W. and S.W. during summer, and N. during December and January.—*Sailing Directions*, by Findlay, p. 506. Mr. Smith marks out on his map his assumed tacking of the vessel on the *north* side of the island. They sailed "*under* Cyprus." "Lee" is that part towards which the wind blows, as opposed to that from which it proceeds.—*Ogilvie's Dictionary.* "'Lee,' a place sheltered *from* the wind by an intervening object, as a bluff: the side of anything opposite to that from which the wind blows."— *Dana (Worcester's Dictionary).* Therefore, they did not go north of the island, for they desired to be sheltered from the wind, which was opposed to their coasting to the north.—T. F.]

[h] This mode of expression was probably derived from the visible elevation of the North Pole of the heavens in northern latitudes. See what is said on this subject in the following part of this Dissertation, of their sailing under Crete, which undoubtedly means on the south side of that island.

[i] [When St. Paul sailed in a vessel of Adramyttium, though it stopped at Myra, it may be presumed to have been on its course to Adramyttium. The intended journey, then, would have been across Macedonia to Dyrrachium. If so, the distinction between the Sea of Adria and the southern or Ionian Sea must have been as perfectly well known to the company on their route to Rome. It may be said, however, the vessel, when hired, was known only to be about to sail along the coasts of Asia, and that, therefore, a change to another vessel was expected, and the whole route was intended to be by sea; or, the land route might have become impracticable in the advanced season when they reached Myra. Mr. Smith thought they sailed north of the island—1. Because, in the fifth verse, the translation of the word διαπλεύσαντες is not sailing "*over*," as interpreted in the Authorized version, but "*sailing through* the sea of Cilicia;" and that they would have avoided this sea if they had sailed *south* of the island. The correct meaning given to the word in Liddell and Scott's *Dictionary* is, "*sailing across*." 2. That there is a constant current westward from Syria to the Archipelago (Beaufort's *Asia Minor*, p. 39), and that by going north they *might* have been favoured by this current and a *northerly* land-wind. These were very feeble and idle suggestions. Having touched at Sidon, the probability is that they were prevented going further up on the coast, north, and so went south of Cyprus. The current would be in their favour. What occurred to prevent their going north disappointed them—*i.e.* something unexpected—that is, if they intended to go north, they were checked by bad weather, namely, "the winds were contrary." By going from the west side of Cyprus to Myra they would have "*sailed across the sea*" of Cilicia and Pamphylia. See the Map of Asia Minor, published by the Society for the Diffusion of Useful Knowledge, which was corrected by the late Admiral Beaufort himself.—T. F.]

Ver. 5.

Ver. 6.

Cyprus, must have been 36° to the north of the west point, crossing both the western part of the Aulon Cilicius and the sea which bounds Pamphylia to the south. Following this course, they arrived at Myra,[k] a sea-port on the coast of Lycia, situated in about 36° 9' N. lat. and 29° 52' E. long. How long they remained at Myra does not appear; probably not long, as they found an Alexandrian ship there, which was bound to Italy, and, as it seems, to Puteoli. The season of the year being advanced, it may be presumed that they would not wait longer than was necessary. As Myra lies nearly under the same meridian with Alexandria [31° 11·5' N. lat. and 29° 51·5' E. long.], it was, from the facility of reaching it, the usual place for the Egyptian corn-ships to touch at in their way to Italy. In the state of navigation at that time it could scarcely be supposed that they would accomplish the voyage from Egypt to Puteoli, without some supplies on the way, both of necessaries, and also of information respecting their course and situation.

Ver. 7.

Their course from Myra appears to have been at first nearly west, with a small deviation to the south, and probably coasting until they came over against or into the meridian of Cnidus, a maritime city of Caria, lying in 36° 41' N. lat. and 27° 24' E. long.[1]

---

[k] [There is a view of Myra in *Travels in Lycia, Milaris, and Cibaratis*, by Capt. T. A. Spratt, R.N., F.R.S., F.G.S., and Professor E. Forbes, F.G.S., 1847, vol. i. "The ruins of Myra are most interesting, but are well known. The theatre is situated at the western edge of the plain at the foot of the mountain, and close to a fine group of rock tombs. It is an immense building, the diameter of which, according to Mr. Cockerell, is 360 feet."—*Newton's Levant*, vol. i. p. 342.—T. F.]

[1] [An interesting account of Rhodes, with views and an excellent map, are to be found in Newton's *Travels in the Levant*. See also Cramer's *Asia Minor*, vol. ii. p. 224.—T. F.]

[The distance from Myra to Cnidus is estimated at 153 geographical miles. Cape Krio, the ancient *Triopium Promontorium*, is the extremity of an extensive promontory, projecting from the mainland of Caria. It is in latitude 36° 40' 56" north, and longitude 27° 24' 0" east. Within Cape Krio [*Tekir*] are the extensive ruins of CNIDUS; these are situated on the side of a mountain, rising gradually from the sea to the height of 400 feet; they are called by the native Greeks, Phrianon. The peninsula of Cape Krio consists of lofty mountains, sloping steeply upwards from the port; but to the westward, facing the sea, it presents a craggy, perpendicular face of rock, from 100 to 300 feet high, and utterly inaccessible.—*Sailing Directions*, p. 324; and see Newton's *Travels*,

So far they had followed the coast as nearly as seems to have been convenient; but here they met with a contrary wind, probably from a northerly quarter,[m] which drove them southward towards Cape Samonium, or Salmone, the eastern promontory of the isle of Crete, and in latitude 35° 9′ N. and in longitude Ver. 7. 26° 19′ E.[n] This promontory they passed in sailing to the

vol. ii. p. 168; and the article "Cnidus" in Smith's *Dictionary of Greek and Roman Geography.*—T. F.]

[m] ["Cape Salmone, the eastern point of Candia, lies in latitude 35° 7·2′ north, and longitude 26° 19′ 25″ east. It is high land, which continues southward to Cape Xarco. This forms the S.E. point of Candia. The southern coast of Candia is altogether high and steep, being in some places inaccessible. From Cape Gialo to Cape Matala, 34° 55′ N. lat., 24° 45·2′ E. long., the course and distance are W. by N., nearly 65 miles. Within this space there is no harbour or place of shelter for shipping to run into. W. ½ N. from Cape Matala, distant 32 miles, is the Island Gozo (Clauda), being 4½ miles in length, and not 2 in breadth. It is elevated, and the shores are all rocky; but there is deep water close in, and no danger. From Cape Matala to Cape Krio the course and distance are W.N.W. ¾ N., 64 miles. Neither the Bay of Messara nor the Port of Spakia affords either safety or shelter. Cape Krio, the S.W. extremity of Candia, is in latitude 35° 15′ 45″ north, and longitude 23° 32′ 35″ east. The channel between Cape Buso and the island Cerigotto is 18 miles wide, with very deep water in it, but free from danger. It is, therefore, the most common and best passage into the Archipelago."—*Sailing Directions.* "The island of Great Gozzo (Clauda) is very high, and may be seen about 40 miles. There is water near the N.E. part of the island, and a *dangerous shoal lying off the south point.* The cliffs on the western part appear to be perpendicular to the sea-coast, and at least 700 feet high."—*Findley's S. D.* 276. Dr. Pocock, in 1739, stated that the road for shipping was to the north. (*Travels,* vol. ii. p. 240.) Capt. Spratt says the island is higher than Malta, its altitude being nearly 1000 feet. The south coast is straight and high, forming a continuous precipice. Capt. Spratt, also, says, "The island has been generally dreaded by the mariner, from its supposed outlying dangers, but the south shore is quite free, being bold and precipitous. It has probably arisen from the passage in Acts xxvii. 17, when the sailors apprehended falling into quicksands. No other danger than the rocks above described exist around it, and none certainly of the nature of quicksands. Nevertheless, the natives have a tradition a shoal was known to their ancestors." The island may, therefore, be boldly approached, and the shelter of its lee, or the anchorage its roadstead affords, be taken advantage of during a *south-west* or *westerly* gale."—*Sailing Directions of the Coast of Candia,* by Capt. Spratt, 2nd edition, revised by Capt. Penn, 1866. Printed for the Hydrographic Office, Admiralty. —*Crete,* vol. ii. p. 275. T. F.]

[n] [Mr. Smith (p. 76) held the wind to have been between W.N.W. and N.N.W., or what, in common language, would be termed North-West. He says, "That with north-west winds the ship could work up from Myra to

southward, and perhaps not without some difficulty,° or danger, and arrived at the Fair Havens,ᵖ situate on the southern side of the same island, nigh whereunto was the city of Lasea.�q

---

Cnidus, having the advantage of a weather shore, under the lee of which she would have smooth water and the westerly current; that when at Cnidus these advantages ceased, and unless she had put into that harbour, and waited for a westerly wind, the only course was to run under the lee of Crete."—T. F.]

° " μόλις τε παραλεγόμενοι αὐτήν—eam ægre prætervecti."—*Schleusneri Lexicon.* " Adversis ventis usi essemus, tardeque et incommode navigâssemus."—*Cicero ad Famil.* lib. xiv. epist. 5.

ᵖ [Dr. Pococke, who was in Candia in July, 1739, stated that there is a small bay about two leagues east of Matala, which was called by the Greeks Λιμνίωνες καλούς, and not far from the site of the city of Lysia in the Peutingerian Tables, which must have been the same with Lasea; and Dr. Pococke placed it about three miles south of a large convent called " Penaia Egetria," but he observed no ruins.—*Pococke's Travels,* vol. ii. p. 250. See Capt. Spratt, R.N., on *Crete,* vol. ii. p. 2. Rochette's Map has a place called " Sancti Limni," nearly in the same spot with that described by Dr. Pococke. " Locus adhuc hodie in Creta nomen retinet, CALOS LIMENAS."—*Wetstein, Note on Acts* xxvii. 8. The chart of Kalos Limniones, published by the Admiralty, has engraved on it " Surveyed by E. W. Brooker, Master R.N., 1852," and it marks the locality of Lasea or Thalassa. St. Paul's Island, in the Bay, is marked 34° 55′ 21″ N. lat. and 24° 49′ 18″ E. long. Mr. Smith (p. 81, n.) ascribed the discovery of Lasea to the Rev. G. Brown, in the year 1856!!—T. F.]

q [Capt. Spratt, R.N.—" The only name of the locality, however, is simply ' the Metoki,' or farm, it being the only cultivated spot for several miles."

" Surprised at thus accidentally discovering the ancient mole, I was also surprised to find on the *cultivated terraces* some *vestiges of ancient buildings,* and, near the beach under them, *a massive piece of Roman wall with brickwork* which seems to have been part of a sea defence, or facing, to support the embankment there. For *none of the priests* of the neighbouring monastery, *nor any of the natives,* had told me of such remains, although I had made frequent inquiries. Doubtless, then, this must be the site of LASEA, the Thelassea of some later transcribers:—thus accidentally discovered after I had sought in vain for it elsewhere, not expecting to find it so near the Haven." —Capt. Spratt's *Crete,* 1865, vol. ii. p. 8. Capt. Spratt was at Lutro in 1853, and again when he finished the survey, in July, 1859. Before he was there the second time, he printed a communication addressed to the late Col. Leake on Lutro, to which the Rev. G. Brown referred [Smith, p. 253] in his letter dated Jan. 1856.—Capt. Spratt on *Crete,* vol. ii. p. 252, whose accuracy is unquestionable. " The ruins of this city " [Lasea], said Mr. Smith, " have been discovered by my friend and relative, the Rev. George Brown!"—*Smith,* p. 81, n.; and see the extraordinary remarks of the Rev. Dr. David Brown, in vol. vi. (Acts xxvii.) of a Bible published by Collins and Co., Glasgow, 1870, on this subject.

The Rev. George Brown.—" Just after we passed Cape Leonda, Miss T.'s quick eye discovered two white pillars standing on an eminence near the shore.

They here found that much time had been already spent or wasted during the voyage, and that the proper season for sailing Ver. 9. had elapsed, the Fast having been for some time passed, and navigation becoming dangerous, of which they were admonished by St. Paul. The master of the ship, however, though conscious that it was not prudent to proceed on his voyage at that season, Ver. 11. was nevertheless desirous to gain a more commodious harbour Ver. 12. to winter in, and undertook to carry the vessel as far as *Phœnice*, a port described by both Ptolemy and Strabo, lying on the southern coast of the island of Crete, and opposite to the small island of *Gaudos*, or *Clauda*, [Ptol. iii. 17. 611; Mela, ii. 7; Plin. iv. 12. s. 20, now called Gozzo;] latitude 34° 47′ 12″ N., longitude 24° 35′ E., and about 50 miles westward of the Fair Havens.

A place in Crete opposite to Gaudos is found in Rochette's Map of Greece and the Archipelago, called Finichia,[r] which was undoubtedly the Phœnice mentioned by St. Luke. It is not easy to determine the exact import of this passage. The words in the original are Λιμένα βλέποντα κατὰ Λίβα καὶ κατὰ Χῶρον, which implies, "open to both those quarters of the

---

Down went the helm, and putting the vessel round, we stood in close, wore, and hove-to. Mr. H. Tennant and I landed immediately, just inside the Cape to the westward, and found the beach lined with masses of masonry." " ABOVE we found the ruins of two temples, &c." "Some *peasants* came down to see us from the hills above, and I asked them the name of the place. They said *at once* LASEA, so there could be no doubt." Mr. Tennant had sailed, in fact, straight to it. This statement of the Rev. George Brown is contained in a letter dated January 15, 1856, and is printed by Mr. Smith, third edition, 1866, p. 260. *Peasants*, on their landing, were immediately met with who identified the ancient ruins, and gave the name of the place, which was unknown to the *priests* of a neighbouring monastery, and unknown to the natives of whom inquiries were made three years before, when the ancient site of Lasea was ascertained by Capt. Spratt. Instruction must have spread since Capt. Spratt had been there. Mr. Smith also (p. 82) stated that a view taken by Señor Schranz, who had accompanied Mr. Pashley, enabled Messrs. Tennant and Brown to identify "The Fair Havens." There is a remarkably pretty view of "The Fair Havens," and of the site of "Lasea," in the second volume of Capt. Spratt's *Crete*, which proves how easily "The Fair Havens" can be identified.—T. F.]

[r] ["Ab Apolloniade ad Phœnicem, stadia 100 : urbs est cum portu *et insula.* A Clauda ad Phœnicem stadia 300 ; habet urbem et portum." *Anonymi Stadiasmus sive Periplus Maris Magni.—Geographi Græci Minores,* vol. ii. p. 496. *Parisiis.* 1828. T. F.]

heavens from whence these winds proceed," and of course unsheltered from the force of these winds. According to Pliny's
arrangement of the winds, this port was exposed to blasts from
the S.W. by W. $\frac{1}{4}$ W. to N.W. by W. $\frac{1}{4}$ W., comprehending
80 degrees, or more than seven points of the compass. If
reckoned according to the arrangement of Vitruvius, it com-
prehends 105 degrees from S.W. to N.N.W. $\frac{1}{4}$ N., being nearly
nine points of the compass.[s]

It might require some explanation why those who navigated
the vessel in which St. Paul was a passenger, chose to pass
round to the south of Cape Salmone, and that not without some
difficulty and hazard, rather than to attempt to put in at
some port on the northern side of Crete. But this question

---

[s] [St. Paul, be it observed, did not reach Phœnice. Mr. Smith (p. 86) has
thus cited the above passage: "Dr. Falconer, a man of undoubted learning,
admits that it is not easy to determine the exact import of this passage; but
supposes it to be 'open to both quarters of the heavens from whence these
winds proceed, and, of course, unsheltered from these winds.' He then observes:
'This would, according to Vitruvius, leave 105° open to the west.' Such a
harbour would not be commodious to winter in, and *would not have war-
ranted the attempt which was made to move to it.*" These last words in italics
are cited as if they were taken from the text above, and then there is an argument to confute the assumed statement by showing that the port of Lutro,
or Phœnice, would have been a commodious port. Mr. Smith was not an
accurate writer. All difficulty has been removed since Capt. Spratt, R.N., in
1853, surveyed Lutro. The Rev. George Brown says, "the land [at Lutro]
cannot have risen materially since the Christian era." Capt. Spratt, in
Sailing Directions for the Island of Crete, 2nd edition, 1866, p. 28, says,
"A Turkish schooner of war lay here during a part of the winter of 1858,
and found that the squalls with N. and N.E. gales were the most to be apprehended and guarded against. The south winds, as above stated, sent in only
a swell, and never fetched home. The vessel bearing St. Paul with her 276
men might thus have wintered in safety in Lutro, as was intended, and this
fact confirms it as being the ancient Phœnice of the Acts, which the captain
of the ship hoped to reach after starting from Fair Havens or Kalos-Limniones.
In those days, also, the depths within the bay must have been two fathoms
greater, and its shore came in a few yards wider and deeper; for notwithstanding my assertion of an elevation of its coast to that amount has been
disputed, I am enabled, by a still more recent visit, to re-assert the fact, and
to maintain it. H.M.S. *Cambrian* lay two or three days in this port in 1827."
"*Phœnice urbs est cum portu et insula.*" This island, close upon the port,
with access to the port on either side of this island, and the line of the channels
of navigation, each open to a different quarter, give the solution of an old difficulty.—T. F.]

is resolved by the account of Eustathius,[t] who on another occasion mentions that there were no good ports on the northern side of that island.[u] The propriety of the caution given by St. Paul was, however, verified in the attempt of those who navigated the ship to sail from the Fair Havens to Phœnice. For in this short passage, although the weather appeared to be favourable at their setting out, they were soon assailed by a violent tempest from the south-east quarter.[x] At what time of the year this happened, and what was the nature and direction of the wind which occasioned it, will be the next subject of inquiry.

Ver. 14.

It has already been observed, that on their arrival at the Fair Havens they found much time had been spent, to which the slowness of their passage from Myra[y] to the meridian of Cnidus had no doubt contributed; that the Fast was already past, and sailing become dangerous. The word ἤδη, which we translate *already*, bears in this place, I think, a more extensive signification. It probably means that the Fast had been over a considerable or at least an indefinite time, and that sailing had likewise been (as I infer from the repetition of the word ἤδη[z]) for a considerable time, dangerous. The Fast alluded to was undoubtedly the Jewish Fast of Expiation, which was observed on the tenth of the month Tisri, or the twenty-fifth of September, the day on which the autumnal equinox[a] was then computed to fall. Stormy weather at sea was usual about this

Ver. 9.

---

[t] Ἀυσλιμένος ἡ Κρήτη πρὸς τὴν βόρραν. Eustath. ad Odyss. τ′.
Unde Lucanus:
      "... Boreaque urgente carinas Creta fugit."—Lib. ix.

[u] [Mr. Smith (p. 81) says that this reason fails, because "there are two excellent harbours on the northern side of Crete, namely, Souda, [35° 30′ N. lat. and 24° 4′ long.] and Spina Longa" [not named in Raper's maritime positions]. He says "that Eustathius, who lived at the beginning of the fourth century, has misled writers."—T. F.]

[x] [Capt. Spratt thinks the wind blew N. by compass, that is, N. 10° W. true: being the invariable direction of a gale in that locality, both in winter and summer.—*Crete*, p. 18. But a good authority objects to the word "invariable" as being opposed to his own experience.—T. F.]

[y] Andriace, the ancient port of Myra, was recognized by Admiral Beaufort to be at the Bay of Audraki.—*Travels in Lydia*, by Capt. Spratt and Professor Forbes, vol. i. p. 134.

[z] "ἤδη e præterito significat rem paratam et peractam sine termino."— *Schleusneri Lexicon.*—"*by this time ;*" "*before this ;*" "*some time before this.*"

[a] Colum. lib. xi. cap. 2.

season; but I am of opinion that the time of this Voyage, and
of course of the Shipwreck, was considerably later in the year
than the Fast, and probably took place towards the end of
November, or the beginning of December.

It appears from Josephus,[b] that navigation was accounted
dangerous among the Jews from the time of the Feast of
Tabernacles, October the first, to that of the Dedication of
the Temple, December the ninth; and in this interval both the
Voyage and Shipwreck probably took place. Vegetius assigns
the third of the Ides[c] (November the eleventh) for the day on
which navigation was interrupted; and we are informed by
the Calendar of Geminus, and by Theophrastus, that stormy
weather at sea may be expected about that season. The day
above specified had, I think, elapsed some time before they left
the Fair Havens, which would nearly correspond with the cosmical[d] setting of Orion (November the ninth), a time of year
remarkable[e] for stormy weather in the seas the vessel which
carried St. Paul was then traversing. Some days more might
pass between the time of the delivery of the caution given
by St. Paul and their setting sail. Fourteen or fifteen days
more were, we know, spent in the Voyage, which brings the
time, without any strain on the narrative, to the end of
November, or the beginning of the succeeding month.

[Cicero (B.C. 50) sailed from Patræ, a town of Achaia (38° 14′
N. lat. and 21° 44′ E. long.), on November 2, and reached Corcyra on the 9th, but he did not make the coast of Italy (*retenti
ventis*) until November 24, when he reached Hydruntum
(*Otranto*), and on the next day (25th) was at Brundusium : being
a detention of many days before he could cross the sea. (*Ad
Fam.* xvi. 9. Long's *Decline of the Roman Empire*, vol. iv.
p. 429.) The duration of the bad weather of St. Paul's Voyage
was fourteen days.[f]

---

[b] See Wetstein's note on this passage. [J. J. Wetstein was born at Basle,
in 1693, and died at Amsterdam in 1754. "His edition of the Greek New
Testament was regarded to be the most elaborate and valuable of all critical
editions."]

[c] "Ex die igitur tertio Iduum Novembris, usque in diem sextum Iduum
Martiarum, *maria clauduntur*."—*Veget.* iv. c. 39.

[d] Plin. xviii. 31.   [e] Virg. Æneid, vii. 719.

[f] Mr. Greswell mentions the instance of Aristides (the orator) being driven

The Emperor Augustus, towards the winter, on his passage to
Italy, met with two violent storms, the first between the promontories of Peloponnesus and Ætolia, and the other about the
Ceraunian mountains, in both of which part of his Liburnian
squadron was sunk; the tackling (*armamenta*) of his own ship
was carried away, and the rudder broken.—*Suetonius, " Cæsar
Augustus,"* ch. 17. At the time when Titus Cæsar besieged
Jerusalem, Vespasian (A.D. 69) embarked in a merchant vessel,
and crossed over from Alexandria to Rhodes. From thence
he sailed, and touched at all the towns in his course, and
being everywhere cordially received, he passed from Ionia into
Greece, and thence from Corcyra to the Iapygian promontory,
whence he pursued his journey by land. — *Josephus, Hist.,*
Traill's trans., bk. vii. ch. 2, p. 475, ed. 1868. He had waited
at Alexandria for the periodical return of the summer gales,
and for settled weather at sea.—*Tacitus, Hist.* bk. iv. ch. 81.
When Titus Cæsar returned from the East, he arrived first at
Rhegium, and from thence sailed in a merchant ship to Puteoli.
—*Suetonius, " Titus,"* ch. 5. Josephus speaking of Herod, says
that, " deterred neither by the circumstances that it was the
depth of winter, nor by the disturbed state of affairs in Italy,
he set sail from Alexandria for Rome. Being in danger near
Pamphylia, he with difficulty and after throwing out the greater
part of the cargo, reached Rhodes, which had suffered severely
in the war with Cassius. He was kindly received by his friends,
Ptolemy and Sapphinius, and having, though in want of money,
fitted out a trireme of the largest class, he and his party embarked in it for Brundusium, whence he hastened to Rome."—
Josephus, Hist., Traill's trans., bk. i. ch. 15, p. 126. They
coasted, as St. Paul did, towards Pamphylia, then were driven
through stress of winter storms to Rhodes, and in another ship
sailed to Brindisi.

" So late as the year 1569, Venice prohibited her vessels,
under heavy penalties, from attempting to return home between
the 15th of November and the 20th of January."—*Admiral
Smyth* on " *The Mediterranean*," p. 255, 8vo, 1854.

---

fourteen days and nights during a gale in the Ægean Sea.—*Dissertations*,
vol. iv. p. 197. Τέτταρες πάλιν αὐταὶ πρὸς ταῖς ἡμέραι δέκα καὶ νύκτες χειμῶνος
κύκλῳ διὰ παντὸς τοῦ πελάγους φερομένων.—See *Smith,* 146, n.

The following notices appeared in 1869 in the public papers:
"*Ministère de la Marine, Bulletin Météorologique* du 29 no-
vembre 1869, 1 heure après-midi.—Fortes tempêtes dans la
Méditerranée, produites par le vent de sud-ouest. Le baro-
mètre a baissé de 1 à 9 millimètres. Il a plu dans quelques
stations."

"*Ship and Mail News.—Brindisi*, Dec. 2, 1869.—The steamer
'Brindisi,' from Alexandria, has arrived here. She experienced severe and contrary winds."

It is, therefore, evident that for nineteen hundred years at least
the November weather, on the eastern coast of the Ionian Sea,
has remained subject to the same influences.—T. F.]

THE WINDS.

Ver. 14.
I shall now speak a few words respecting the wind which
caused this tempest. The Latin Vulgate translation, that of
Castalio, and some others, render the word "*Euroclydon*" by
"*Euro-aquilo*,"⁶ a word found nowhere else, and inconsistent, as
I think, in its construction with the principles on which the
names of the intermediate or compound winds are framed.
Euronotus is so called, as intervening immediately between
Eurus and Notus, and as partaking, as was thought, of the
qualities of both. The same holds true of Libonotus, as being
interposed between Libs and Notus. Both these compound
winds lie in the same quarter or quadrant of the circle with
the winds of which they were composed, and no other wind
intervenes.

But Eurus and Aquilo are at 90° distance from one another;
or, according to some writers, at 15° more, *i.e.* at 105°; the
former lying in the south-east quarter, and the latter in
the north-east; and two winds, one of which is the East car-
dinal point, intervene, as Cœcias and Subsolanus. The Carbas
of Vitruvius occupies a middle point between Eurus and Aquilo
in his scheme of the winds; but this never had, nor could have,

---

⁶ See Rev. Dr. Shaw concerning this wind (*Travels*, 3rd ed. p. 131). He
says that haziness of the atmosphere, or a great accumulation of clouds which,
to use the mariners' phrase, frequently *hang*, without dissipating, for several
days together *in the East wind's eye*, are common to "Levanters."

the appellation of Euro-aquilo, as it lies in a different quarter, and the East point is interposed, which could scarcely have been overlooked in the framing a compound appellation. The word Euroclydon is evidently composed of Eurus, or Εὖρος, the south-east wind, and κλύδων, a wave, an addition highly expressive of the character and effects of this wind,[h] but probably chiefly

---

[h] [The most remarkable modern illustration of the Voyage of St. Paul is to be found in the *Travels and Researches in Crete*, vol. ii. p. 11, 1865. The professional and scientific knowledge of the author, Capt. Spratt, R.N., C.B., F.R.S., entitles his opinion to be received with the utmost respect. It appears that, being at the " Fair Havens," a gale from the *south-east* (*Eurus*) compelled him to put to sea, and to remain in the offing for twenty-four hours till it had veered round, as usual, to the south-west, when the sea abated, and he returned. He put to sea again when it was apparently calm enough, tempted by a calm morning, in order to reach the Bay of Messara. Part of his "course" was just that which the captain of St. Paul's ship desired to steer in making for the port of Phœnice to the south-west of Crete (against the advice of St. Paul), since, to reach this port, it was necessary to sail rather close to the Cretan coast. "When the south wind blew softly," supposing they had obtained their purpose, " loosing thence they sailed close by Crete." "Thus the captain of the Alexandrian ship being dependent on *fair winds* in those days (as are the junks of the Chinese in the present,—which his ship must have somewhat resembled in rig and form), he was tempted to loose from ' Fair Havens' on experiencing a light southerly wind in that port, and to proceed on this route for Phœnice— exactly as we were also tempted by a calm and still morning after a southerly gale to sail from it for the head of Messara Bay." Capt. S. then describes light cat's-paws on the sea, sometimes from the north and sometimes from the south, the sky being bright and clear, the rising of the storm on getting round Cape Littinos into Messara Bay, until it blew a perfect hurricane from the north; the white spoon-drift occasionally covered the bay as a sheet of foam, or rose as a whirling column of spray, dashing over the bows and bulwarks, and wetting all, fore and aft, the wind blowing direct from Mount Ida to Cape Littinos.—*Crete*, vol. ii. p. 14. "We had in all probability, under nearly similar circumstances, in respect to the *character*, force, and direction of the wind, encountered 'a Euroclydon,'—the very wind which proved so disastrous to St. Paul's ship on attempting to cross the bay for the western harbour of Phœnice, and which has given rise to so much difficulty and to so many learned dissertations upon the meaning of the term by scholars and commentators upon the voyage and shipwreck of the great Apostle, most of whom have concluded that the *direction* and not the *character* of the wind was intended by the word ' Euroclydon' in St. Luke's record of its effect on the ship. [Capt. S., when he printed this, had not seen the above text of the Dissertation.] The impression that we were encountering this very wind naturally struck me at the time, for a long experience of the winds of the Levant enables me to state that, as in most other places, this locality (that is, the Greek Archipelago and Crete) has its peculiar local winds, the most violent and the most constant being from

applied to it when it became typhonic[1] or tempestuous. Indeed, the general character under which Eurus, or the South-
East wind, is described agrees with the description of the effects
of the wind which caused the distress related in the account of
this voyage.

[In fact, even if it be held to have been an error of the tran-
scriber, "Euroclydon" was a very appropriate term, and the
combination of words in "Euro-aquilo" is perfectly inexpli-
cable from the distance from each other of these two points of
wind (see Table of Winds), unless expressive of a changeable
state of winds. The Very Rev. Dean Howson (*Life of St. Paul*,
ed. 1868, vol. ii. p. 346) says: "We have a strong impression

---

certain points only. The 'meltem' [a local term known throughout the Archipelago, among Greek and Turkish Levantine sailors, for a violent northerly
gale] is one of them: it generally rises very suddenly, without many clouds
to warn the navigator, some few mountains only being capped by them as
monitors of its coming to the experienced local navigator. It is especially
dreaded for the violence of its squalls on the leeward side of high lands: for
they have the character of what nautical men call 'white squalls,' for giving
little or no warning until felt, and are *truly 'typhonic' in effect from the
whirling* columns of wind and spray they lift from the surface of the sea."
Capt. S. got shelter in Eremopili Bay, but "the 'meltem' lasted three whole
days with unabated fury" (p. 20).—T. F.]

[1] Typhon is described by Pliny as "præcipua navigantium pestis, non
antennas modo verum ipsa navigia contorta frangens."—*Plin.* ii. c. 48. [He
says, also, that the wind Aquilo does not cause it: "*Non fit autem Aquilonius typhon.*"—Lib. ii. ch. 49. T. F.]

["Navigabimus a Cassiopa Brundisium MARE IONIUM violentum et
vastum et jactabundum. Nox deinde, quæ diem primum secuta est, in ea fere
tota ventus a latere sæviens navem undis compleverat. Tum postea complo-
rantibus nostris omnibus atque in sentina satis agentibus, *dies quidem tandem
inluxit.* Sed nihil de periculo neque de sævitia venti remissum, quin turbines
etiam crebriores, et cælum atrum, et fumigantes globi, et figuræ quædam
nubium metuendæ quos 'TYPHONAS' vocabant, impendere imminereque ac
depressuræ navem videbantur."—*Auli Gellii Noct. Att.* lib. xix. ch. 1, p. 219,
ed. Martin Hertz, Leipsic, 1853, Teubner. AULUS GELLIUS lived A.D. 117–140,
and was, therefore, as well as Appian, contemporary with Ptolemy. "The wind
Euroclydon," says Bryant (but not citing his authority), "was certainly a
hurricane. These winds veer round, and blow from every point of the compass;
but at last settle to one particular station from whence they often rage with
no less violence, but more steadfastness, for a long time." Mr. Smith (p. 101, n.)
omits the first sentence when referring to the above passage of Aulus Gellius.
Were the words "*Mare Ionium,*" "a Cassiopa Brundisium" too instructive?
—T. F.]

that *Euroclydon* is the correct reading. The addition of the words '*which was called*' seems to us to show that it was a name popularly given by the sailors to the wind : and nothing is more natural than that St. Luke should use the word which he heard the seamen employ on the occasion. Besides it is the more difficult reading." The Rev. Dr. Shaw, Regius Professor of Greek, Oxford (*Travels*, vol. ii. p. 131, 3rd ed. 1808), also wrote : "We are told this tempestuous [typhonic] wind was *called* ' Euroclydon ; ' the expression seems to suppose it not to have been one of the common winds, such as were entirely denominated from their site and position, but such a one as received its name from some particular quality and circumstance which over and above attended it." It is the word "called" which shows "Euro-Aquilo" may not be a correct reading.—T. F.]

[The readings of the MSS. are :—

> Εὐρακύλων,
> ευρακυλων.
> > *Codex Alexandrinus*,
> > > London, 1860, p. 293.

> εὐρυκλύδων,
> εὐρακύδων.
> > *Codex Vaticanus*,
> > > London, 1859, p. 288.

The *lectio Vaticana Birchii* is εὐρακύλων; and the question has been, whether or not the uncial letter was Λ or Δ. Dr. Tregelles and Dean Alford say the true reading of the Vatican MSS. is Λ ; but either reading only in a small degree affects the argument, unless it can reasonably be inferred the typhonic storm in question was not accompanied with the presumed usual changes of wind.

In the Italian version the word is "Euroclidone ; " in the Spanish, "Euro-aquilon." The Vatican MS. has been tampered with. Some critics say "Εὐρακύδων" was the original reading. Tischendorf says "Εὐρακύλων" was the original. "Error," he says, "might be expected from the fact of the corrector substituting the word ' εὐρυκλύδων ' for ' εὐρακύλων,' altering ' Λ ' into ' Δ,' and adding ' Λ ' after ' Κ.' " The explanation given is unsatisfactory, and a photograph of the words is desirable. It

TABULA VENTORUM secundum Auctores quosdam antiquos et Ventorum Turrim quæ Athenis est ad Pyxidem Nauticam Anglorum accommodata.—W. F., 1810.

		Vitruvius.	Aristoteles.	Plinius.	Vegetius.	Ptolemæus.	Agathemerus.	Geoponica.	Templ. Vent.	Strabo.	Homer.
N.	15°	Septentrio	Απαρκτιας	{Απαρκτιας / Septentrio}	{Απαρκτιας / Septentrio}	Απαρκτιας	Απαρκτιας	Βορεας	Βορεας	Βορεας	Βορεας
		Gallicus									
	30°	Supernas	{Βορεας / Μεσης}	Aquilo	{Βορεας / Aquilo}	Βορεας	Βορεας	Απαρκτιας			
N.E.	45°	Aquilo	Καικιας	Cœcias	Καικιας	Καικιας	Καικιας	Καικιας	Καικιας	Καικιας	
	60°	Βορεας									
	75°	Carbas									
E.	90°	Solanus	Απηλιωτης	Subsolanus	{Απηλιωτης / Subsolanus}	Απηλιωτης	Απηλιωτης	Απηλιωτης	Απηλιωτης	Απηλιωτης	Ευρος
	105°	Ornithiæ									
	120°	Cœcias	Ευρος	Eurus	{Ευρος / Vulturnus}	Ευρος	Ευρος	Ευρος			
S.E.	135°	Etrus		Euronotus					Ευρος	Ευρος	
	150°	Vulturnus	Ευρονοτος		{Λευκονοτος / Albus Notus}	Ευρονοτος	Ευρονοτος	Ευρονοτος			
	165°	{Leuconotus / Euronotus}									
S.	180°	{Nolus / Auster}	Νοτος	Auster	{Νοτος / Auster}	Νοτος	Νοτος	Νοτος	Νοτος	Νοτος	Νοτος
		1	2	3	4	5	6	7	8	9	10

		1	2	3	4	5	6	7	8	9	10
	195°	Altanus									
	210°	Libonotus	Λιβονοτος	Libonotus	{Λιβονοτος / Corus}	Λιβονοτος	Λιβονοτος	Λιβονοτος			
S.W.	225°	Africus	Λιψ	Africus	{Λιψ / Africus}	Λιψ	Λιψ	Λιψ	Λιψ	Λιψ	
	240°	Subvesperus									
	255°	Argestes									
W.	270°	Favonius	Ζεφυρος	Favonius	Ζεφυρος	Ζεφυρος	Ζεφυρος	Ζεφυρος	Ζεφυρος	Ζεφυρος	Ζεφυρος
	285°	Etesiæ									
	300°	Circius	Αργεστης	Corus	{Ιαπυξ / Favonius}	Αργεστης	Ιαπυξ	Ιαπυξ	Σκιρων	Αργεστης	
N.W.	315°	Caurus									
	330°	Corus	Θρασκιας	Thrascias	{Θρασκιας / Circius}	Θρασκιας	{Θρασκιας / Μεσης}	Θρασκιας			
	345°	Thrascias									
N.	360°										

Aulus Gellius [Lug. Bat. 1664, p. 161, lib. ii. cap. 22] says: "Hi sunt, igitur, tres venti orientales, *Aquilo*, *Vulturnus*, *Eurus*, quorum medius *Eurus* est," and see the remarks by Mr. Bryant on Gellius [p. 337], who does *not* use the word Euro-aquilo as represented at page 266 of Mr. Smith's work. Observe, also, the authors who do not use the word "Aquilo." "Who," says Mr. Bryant, "could imagine there would ever be a controversy about the particular stations of the Greek winds so long as the Temple of the Winds at Athens exists?" "*Non fit autem Aquilonius typhon.*"—Plin. lib. ii. ch. 49.

C

is said, also, that ' A ' was converted into ' T,' and after ' K ' was inserted ' A,' and then the Greek uncial letter Λ was converted into Δ. How was the space found for the ' Λ ' which follows ' K '? But let it be admitted the word is " Euro-aquilo," what wind does this word represent? If the reader will turn to the Table of the Winds (p. 20), he will see that the writers of authority, named in the table, place the wind Aquilo, north-east, and the same writers place the wind Eurus some 30 degrees south of east. What wind can such a combination as Euro-aquilo denote? E.N.E. or N.E., say some persons. This would be an Aquilo wind, and the wind Eurus—south of east—would be suppressed. The word Aquilo, without Eurus, would give a similar result. But even an E.N.E. wind was not enough to satisfy Mr. Smith's theory, and therefore, said Mr. S., the seamen set " storm sails" (pp. 110, 113). Without sails on the vessel his explanation of the word Euro-aquilo would be of no avail, for how otherwise could his E.N.E. wind have driven the vessel, in a direct course, east to west, from Clauda to Malta? The necessity of sails being admitted, in order to sustain the interpretation founded on it, is self-destructive of the argument, for we are not authorized to make this addition to the narrative, though we may make probable inferences. The proposed addition would be contradictory of what is said by St. Luke. Mr. Bryant (vol. v. p. 352, ed. 1807) argued this question exceedingly well. It is said, that Euro-aquilo means an E.N.E. wind, or, in round terms, a N.E. wind. Construe it so, and see what sense can be made of it:—" In a short time there beat upon it a typhonic wind called a N.E. wind." The *species* (the typhonic wind) is said to be denominated by the genus,—the " north-east wind." The fact of the designation being simply *particular* and not *general* is especially marked by the use of the word " called." A general denomination does not specify or distinguish. The N.E. wind may blow at any time, but a N.E. wind is not "called" or known as a " typhonic" wind. A particular and unusual tempestuous or " typhonic " wind, when it blew, was called " Euroclydon." It is not said, that when the usual wind called " north-east" blew, it was "typhonic or tempestuous." Those who affirm that the true reading is Euroaquilo, are also obliged, for their purpose, to manipulate the word, and to make it "Aquilo-euro." Even then, they are in a difficulty, for the word "Eurus" did not designate the east but a south-east wind. "Aquilo," also, is not a Greek name, and it alone denotes a north-east wind. Yet it is inferred that Greek or Latin seamen compounded a Latin general term designating the north-east with a general Greek term designating the south-east, in order to designate a *particular* and typhonic wind. The compound term "Euroclydon" is free from all difficulties. The word "Euroclydon" may have been in an early manuscript. It certainly correctly describes the effect of what occurred, namely, a typhonic storm, and itself explains why the word "called" was used. Probably the wind, in *the first instance,* came from the south-east, and then became variable, as is said to be the case in typhonic storms which Pliny stated, "the N.E. wind (Aquilo) did not cause."—T. F. and B.]

I. Eurus raises great waves.

Virgil, in his account of the storm which destroyed a part of the fleet of Æneas in the same seas, enumerates Eurus among the winds, qui

"... vastos volvunt ad littora fluctus."—*Æneid,* i. 86.

Again :

"Aut, ubi navigiis violentior incidit *Eurus,*
Nosse, quot Ioxii veniant ad littora fluctus."
Virg. Georg. ii. 107, 108.

"Quam multi Libyco volvuntur marmore fluctus,
Sævus ubi Orion hibernis conditur undis."[k]

"... ubi nubifer Eurus [S.E.]
Naufragium spargens operit freta."
Silius Italicus, x. 323, 324.

Horace mentions the effects of this wind in terms nearly similar.

"Niger rudentes Eurus, inverso mari,
Fractosque remos differat.
Insurgat Aquilo [N.E.], quantus altis montibus
Frangit trementes ilices."—*Horat. Epod.* x. 5.

Particularly in the Sicilian and Italian seas.

"... Eurus
Per Siculas equitavit undas."—*Carm.* iv. 4, 43.

---

[k] Æneid, vii. 718, 719. The sword of Orion begins to set on the 22nd of Scorpio (Nov. 9).—*Plin.* xviii. 31.

* " . . . quodcunque minabitur Eurus
Fluctibus Hesperiis."—*Carm.* i. 28, 25.

II. Eurus brings dark cloudy weather.
It is called "niger Eurus" by Horace, who also says,

" Nec sidus atra nocte amicum appareat,
Qua tristis Orion cadit."—*Horat. Epod.* x. 9.

III. A combination of Eurus with Notus seems to have been
very destructive in the Mediterranean Sea.

" Una Eurusque [S.E.] Notusque [S.] ruunt creberque procellis
Africus " [S.W.]—*Virg. Æneid,* i. 85.

" Ut horridis utrumque verberes latus
Auster, memento fluctibus;
Niger rudentes Eurus, inverso mari,
Fractosque remos differat."—*Horat. Epod.* x. 3.

" Inter utrumque fremunt immani turbine venti
Nescit, cui domino pareat, unda maris.
Nam modo purpureo vires capit Eurus ab ortu :
Nunc *Zephyrus* sero vespere missus, adest,
Nunc gelidus sicca *Boreas* [1] bacchatur ab Arcto,
Nunc Notus adversa proelia fronte gerit."
Ovid. Trist. lib. i. El. ii. 25.

" Sæpe per Ionium Libycumque natantibus ire
Interjunctus equis omnesque assuetus in oras
Cæruleum deferre patrem : stupuere relicta
Nubila, certantes *Eurique Notique* sequuntur."
Statii Thebaid. lib. vi. 307.

IV. The south-west wind in winter was a wind that was feared :

" Africus furibundus ac ruens ab occidente hiberno."
Seneca, Nat. Quæst. 5.

" Luctantem Icariis fluctibus *Africum*
Mercator metuens."—*Horat. Carm.* i. 1.

---

[1] [Arrian relates that soon after setting sail from Athenæ Ponticæ, the wind
Βορρᾶς calmed the sea. A similar effect is ascribed to it by other Eastern
writers. Thus it is said in the Book of Job (ch. xxxvii. 22) that "fair
weather cometh out of the North ;" and in the Proverbs that, " The North
wind driveth *away* rain." Boreas is called by Homer (*Iliad,* xv. 171 ; xix.
358; *Odyss.* v. 296) Αἰθρηγενέτης, or *serenitatem inducens.* Hippocrates, who
may be regarded much in the same light with Homer as an Oriental writer,
says, "the North-wind produces fair weather and clears the air."—*Dissertation
on Arrian's Voyage of the Euxine Sea,* by W. Falconer, M.D., p. 39, 1805.—
T. F.]

V. South or south-east winds were prevalent in the Mediterranean at this season of the year: "Quinto Idus Novembris[m] (Nov. 9) hiemis initium, Auster aut Eurus."

It appears from Columella,[n] that the stormy weather at this time of the year came mostly from a Southern quarter.

Nov.	6	South or west wind.		Nov.	17	South wind.
	8	South-east wind.			18	Stormy.
	9	South-east wind.			20	South wind.
	11	Seas dangerous to sail on.		Dec.	7	South or south-east wind.
	16	South wind.				

VI. Southerly winds were particularly distressful to those who navigated the Adriatic Sea.

> " Qua tristes Hyadas,[o] nec rabiem Noti;
> Quo non arbiter *Adriæ*
>   Major, tollere seu ponere vult freta.
> Quem mortis timuit gradum
>   Qui siccis oculis monstra natantia
>   Qui vidit mare turgidum et
>   Infames scopulos Acroceraunia?"—*Horat. Carm.* i. 3.

> "Me quoque devexi rapidus comes Orionis
>   *Illyricis* Notus obruit undis."—*Ibid.* i. 28.

> " . . . neque Auster
> Dux inquieti turbidus *Adriæ*."—*Ibid.* iii. 3.

In another place he alludes to a person driven into the Adriatic Sea by the south wind:

> " . . . Ille Notis actus ad Oricum,[p] [Erikhó]
> Post insana Capræ sidera."—*Ibid.* iii. 7.

VII. The cosmical setting of Capra was, according to Columella, on the tenth of the Calends of January (Dec. 23), and indicated stormy weather. The Greek Calendar of Geminus[q] foretells storms about the same time, and, as it would seem, from a southerly quarter.

---

[m] Columella, xi. 2. [n] Ibidem.

[o] The Hyades set, according to Columella, Nov. 17 and 19; according to Geminus, Nov. 21.

[p] [See in a subsequent page the notice of a similar event in the case of Mr. Galt. Æmilius Paulus embarked his troops at Oricum for Italy after his cruel campaign in the year B.C. 167. The name of the harbour was Panormus. Between Apollonia and Oricum was Aulon (*Avlona*).—T. F.]

[q] Petav. Uranolog.

Dec.			Dec.		
	2	Stormy weather.		26	Stormy.
	5	South wind.		31	South wind.
	6	Storms of thunder, &c.		2	Storms at sea from south.
	11	Stormy.		4	Storms at sea from south.
	20	Stormy.		6	South wind.
	21	Stormy.		15	Stormy.

[It is thought to be advisable for the convenience of the reader here to interpolate, as supplementary to these accounts of the weather given by ancient writers, the modern notices of the winds and currents of those portions of what is now generally called the " Mediterranean Sea," where the ship may have drifted. When this Dissertation was written, such information was very partially obtainable.

1. As respects the currents of the sea.

On the map of Malta and Gozo of A. F. G. de Palmeus, 1799, these words are engraved:—" The currents at the entrance of the Channel on the N. West side set almost constantly to the East-South-East, and on the East-South-East side, they *set to the East.*" Thus the current would carry any vessel drifting in that quarter *towards the east : not from the east to the west* or towards Malta from the east. This fact is very important. The modern sailing directions also state that the current " most commonly sets southward and eastward."[r]

2. Winds and Tides.—As respects the Adriatic, it is said, (*Findlay, S. D.*, 1868, p. 222) :

" In the Ionian Sea, the prevalent winter winds are from the south-south-west to east-south-east." (*Admiral Smyth, " The Mediterranean,"* p. 261.) "The commencement of the Bora, like the *black squall*, is generally indicated by some dark clouds, which rise up with great velocity from the mountains."

"The Bora generally continues three days; and, in an advanced season, it will very often last nine, fifteen, or even so long as *thirty days*, many times subsiding at intervals; during which cessations *it would be highly imprudent for any vessel to*

---

[r] [Mr. William Turner (*Journal of a Tour in the Levant*, 1820, vol. iii. p. 31), when near the island of Ossoro in the Adriatic, Jan. 23, wrote, " All night was a dead calm; but we were carried along by a strong current (that always runs in this sea from the straits between the islands) from twenty-five to thirty miles."—I am told, however, the ordinary current on the Ragusa coast up the Adriatic, is a little more than at the rate of one mile an hour; but the current runs up to and past Meleda.—T. F.]

make sail until the before-mentioned symptoms *have entirely disappeared.*"—*Findlay, S. D.*, 1868, p. 222. ,

"The *S.E.* is a wind which blows with considerable force in the Adriatic, creating an *extremely high* sea, and is accompanied with heavy rains; but then there is this advantage attending it, that vessels at all times will be able to gain the anchorages which the eastern coast affords. *During winter this wind will often last a long while; it usually blows alternately with the Bora,* and during the intervals light and variable breezes may be expected."

"After *the third day* the S.E. wind becomes most dangerous; because the swell of the sea which it raises, *running in the direction of the Adriatic,* progressively acquires a new force, and ends by becoming tremendous. If, from the *haziness of the weather,* the coast *should not be distinguishable,* then your vessel would be in great danger of being driven upon it."

"*This S.E. wind* is commonly preceded by dark clouds, which cover the summits of the mountains and the isles, by a greater rise of water, and by the air being more temperate than usual. The south wind is also announced by similar appearances, and produces the same effect."

"Vessels are dangerously situated when, after having entered the Adriatic, they happen to be driven towards that part of the coast which lies *between Avlona and Ragusa;* for here are no roadsteads in which protection can be readily found. The S.W. and W. winds are not so much to be dreaded, nor the N. and N.W. winds, since they [N. and N.W.] do not create so great a swell of the sea; and besides, if it should not be possible to gain a port, with these winds you can readily run to the southward and *out* of the gulf."

"In summer it will be of advantage for vessels which leave the Adriatic to keep to the N.E. coast, as it generally is subject to heavy N.W. winds, which, during the night and part of the morning, leave light breezes at east. On the contrary, those who enter the gulf ought, during the summer, to keep over the Italian shore, as there are along that coast, during the night and part of the morning, some light land breezes, to which a S.E. wind generally succeeds."

Admiral Smyth says, "the coming on of the Bora may fortunately be known some hours beforehand by a dense, dark cloud on the horizon, with light fleecy clouds above it, a rather lurid sky; and it ,is immediately preceded by a breathless but speaking stillness. Its general source is between north and north-east, and its most usual continuance about fifteen or twenty hours, with heavy squalls, and terrible thunder, lightning, and rain, at intervals; but the Bora most feared, and with justice, is that which blows in sudden gusts for three days, then subsides, and then resumes its former force for three days more. Ships caught in it generally let fly everything to receive the first blast; then immediately bear up to southward, to seek safety in any port they can fetch, or remain under bare poles till it is exhausted."—" *The Mediterranean,*" p. 256. I have been told, however, that the Bora frequently comes on without notice. No doubt it comes on suddenly, apparently suddenly, if not watched for. There is a very descriptive account of the raging of the Bora, p. 258 of "*The Mediterranean,*" by Admiral Smyth.—T. F.]

3. [*Currents.*—The repeated observations of the pilots, and the numerous experiments made for obtaining the right soundings on both coasts, and in the middle part of the Adriatic, *clearly prove at all times* the existence of a general current, which, *running in at the Albanian side,* takes a N.W. direction *along the eastern coast,* turning to S.E. at the bottom of the sea, and running out of it, always sweeping along the Italian shore." Respecting these currents more will be said hereafter under the title "Meleda."—*Sail. Dir. Norie,* p. 124; *Findlay,* 223. The stormy character of a winter in the Adriatic might most certainly have detained the "Castor and Pollux" at Meleda.— T. F.]

4. [Mr. Findlay (p. 166) says:—" The Sirocco, or Sciroc, which at times prevails in a different season of the year, has been noticed as follows by Mr. Galt in his lively volume entitled, *Letters from the Levant.* He sailed *from Malta* [35° 54′ N. lat. and 14° 31′ E. long.] in a Greek polacca belonging to the island of Petza, or Spetzia [37° 15′ N. lat., 23° 8′ E. long.], in the Gulf of Nauplia, 18th January, 1810, for the purpose of proceeding to that place; but on the next forenoon, he says that a Levantine sciroc arose, and continued to increase for

twenty-four hours, while, however, the vessel worked onward. On the morning of the 21st (third day) it blew a perfect hurricane; and the polacca bore away before the wind *for a port in the Adriatic.* At noon the sky appeared to be involved in a thick tumultuous smoke; and the vessel was suspended, as it were, on the curl of a vast wave; and, *although there was as little of the foresail spread as possible,* she drove at a prodigious rate. When in sight of Corfu [39° 40′ N. lat., 19° 41′ E. long.] *the wind shifted* to another quarter, and shelter was at length found in the harbour of Valona or Avlona " [the ancient Aulon,* in lat. 40° 27′].

William Falconer [Mr. Findlay adds] in his *Shipwreck,* has not less *accurately* than finely described these gales, and it would be unwise to reject his description merely because it is in verse. The 'Britannia' on the way between Egypt and Venice, touched at Candia [the north side of Crete], was turned out of the bay, and attempted a passage to the northward:—

> " Fair Candia now no more, beneath her lee
> Protects the vessel from the insulting sea :
> Round her broad arms, impatient of control,
> Roused from their secret deeps the billows roll ;
> Sunk were the bulwarks of the friendly shore,
> And all the scene a hostile aspect wore.

---

* [It has been asked, If St. Paul's ship had been driven in a similar manner, where would it have been at the end of fourteen days ?

> "... Ille Notis actus ad Oricum
> Post insana Capræ sidera."

" The Bay of Avlona is separated from the Adriatic by a rocky promontory, which forms the extremity of the Acroceraunian range, and terminates in a point, 2290 feet high, anciently called 'Glossa' and now 'Linguetta.' ... The ancient port town was 'Oricum' at the bottom of the bay, where some scattered ruins called 'Erico' still attest its site and name. ... Ascending from the valley between the ranges of Longarra and Chika, one enters Khimarra by a narrow plateau called 'Kiafe' (head) which overlooks the sea, and being exposed to the north, south, and west winds, is always approached with apprehension, for sudden squalls, in all seasons, sweep over it with a force neither man nor horse can withstand. Here, also, electric clouds are frequently arrested in their course, and discharge their contents with an effect which shows that the name of 'Acroceraunia' (thunderbolt-point) is no poetic fancy."— *Major R. Stuart on Epirus,* Geogr. Soc. Jour. vol. xxxix., 1869, pp. 277, 278 ; and see also Lear's *Journal in Albania and Illyrica,* pp. 210–213.—T. F.]

The flattering wind that late with promis'd aid
From Candia's bay the unwilling ship betray'd,
No longer fawns beneath the fair disguise,
But like a ruffian on his quarry flies."'—*Line* 221.

" But see! in confluence borne before the blast
Clouds roll'd on clouds, *the dusky noon o'ercast;*
The black'ning ocean curls ; the winds arise ;
And the dark scud in quick succession flies,
While the swol'n canvas bends the mast on high,
Low in the waves the leeward cannon lie.

. . . .

" Still blacker clouds, that all the skies invade,
Draw o'er the sullied orb a dismal shade.
A squall, deep low'ring, blots the *southern* sky,
Before whose boisterous breath the waters fly,
It comes resistless and with foaming sweep,
Upturns the whit'ning surface of the deep;
With ruin pregnant now the clouds impend,
And storm and cataract tumultuous blend."

5. " And when the south wind blew softly," verse 13 :

" But sickening vapours *lull the air to sleep,*
And not a wind awakes the silent deep ;
This when the autumnal equinox is o'er,
And Phœbus in the North declines no more :
The watchful mariner, whom Heaven informs,
Oft deems the prelude of approaching storms."

From these notices of the winds it is utterly impossible to believe that the vessel, when off Crete, was struck "with a point wind—that is, an E.N.E. wind blowing steadily from one point—and that no change took place in its direction during the remainder of the voyage" (*Smith*, p. 101). The true conclusion must be, that from such storms and winds as usually blow at the season of the year when the Voyage occurred, and from the expressions used by St. Luke, no person, seaman or

---

' [I have before me a note and presentation copies of the *Shipwreck*, and of the *Marine Dictionary*, which accompanied it, from Mrs. Jane Falconer the widow of the author, to Dr. William Falconer. The *Shipwreck* contains a map of the course from Candia to Colonna, where the vessel was wrecked. The first entry on the map, after the storm began is, " Ship tears away before the squall." The second entry is, " Again hauls her wind 2 reefed topsails: 3 points lee-way. Wind S. by W." This storm began from the south-west. —T. F.]

not, can affirm what particular wind or winds blew during the fourteen days.—T. F.]

A circumstance little noticed should be mentioned, which is, that St. Luke's words imply that this tempestuous wind drove forcibly ["Ἔβαλε κατ' αὐτῆς ἄνεμος τυφωνικὸς, ὁ καλούμενος Εὐροκλύδων, Acts xxvii. 14] towards the island. I cannot agree with the remark of Schleusner [vox βάλλω] on this passage, who interprets the words κατ' αὐτῆς to mean the ship, when it is evident that they mean the island, from the grammatical construction, and refer to τὴν Κρήτην in the preceding line. Our translation points, though rather obscurely, to the same meaning ["There arose against it"] which is rather more clearly expressed in the Rheims translation ["A tempestuous wind called Euro-aquilo drove against it"]; the Vulgate ["Misit se contra ipsam (Cretam scilicet) ventus typhonicus"] and Castalio's version ["In eam procellosus ventus impegit"] agree in the same explanation.ᵘ

* [I think κατ' αὐτῆς may refer to the ship: though the natural construction would refer to the island. But if the storm commenced from the S.E., which as we are told, was "typhonic," it is not improbable no correction of the words of St. Luke is needed. Mr. Bryant was of opinion the wind beat on the island (p. 354) and that the wind came from S. or S.E. Capt. Spratt suggests another interpretation of the words (Crete, vol. ii. p. 17): "But in truth," he says, "the direction of the typhonic wind experienced by St. Paul seems, to my humble judgment as a navigator, to be explained by St. Luke himself in the words 'there arose against it' [which is the interpretation in our version of the original κατ' αὐτῆς, and no other is needed]; for the course the vessel must steer, to reach Phœnice from Fair Havens, after passing Cape Littinos, was that which was naturally uppermost in the mind of the captain endeavouring to fetch Phœnice; and no doubt St. Luke also, when he wrote, 'there arose against it a tempestuous wind called the Euroclydon,' as appears evident from his having just before noticed that this was 'their purpose' in loosing from Fair Havens with the south wind, as it would carry them on their direct course to Phœnice. I think, moreover, that what St. Luke says in the twelfth verse, in reference to Phœnice,—'which is a haven of Crete and lieth towards the south-west and north-west,'—implies the directions in which the vessel must steer to reach it, viz., towards south-west for some little distance after leaving Fair Havens, and then north-west, after passing Cape Littinos. It seems to me, therefore, that the disputed κατ' αὐτῆς, 'against it,' refers neither to the vessel nor the island of Crete, as generally supposed by previous commentators, but to the direct course to Phœnice. A wind at north, by compass [that is, N. 10° W. true], which I am sure is the invariable [?] direction of a gale in that locality, both in winter and summer, would be adverse to the direct course between Fair Havens and Phœnice after passing Cape Littinos: in fact,

This acceptation of the signification of this passage contradicts the idea that the wind Euroclydon blew from a northerly quarter, as it must in such case have driven the vessel from the island, and not towards it, as it appears to have done. The course of the wind from the south-east would impel the ship towards the island of Crete, though not so directly but that they might have got clear of it. When the ship was caught and could not bear up against the wind they let her drive, running under, or to the south of the island of Clauda or Gaudos, which lies opposite to the port of Phœnice, the place where they purposed to winter.

Ver. 16.

A difficulty occurs in this part of the narrative. Those who navigated the ship were apprehensive of falling among the Syrtes (quicksands) which lay on the coast of Africa, nearly to the south-west of the western point of Crete. But we should consider that this danger lay only in the fears of the mariners, who, knowing the Syrtes to be the great terror of those seas,[x] and probably not being able to ascertain from what quarter the wind blew, as these typhonic Levanters are apt to change their direction,[y] they might have entertained apprehensions that they would be cast on these dangerous quicksands. The event, however, proved that the place of their danger was mistaken.

Ver. 17.

Ver. 20.

[Mr. Bryant (p. 391) uses a very strong argument against the

'against it' for a vessel dependent upon sails such as were then used. That course being N. 60° W. true, would only be 4¼ or 5 points from the wind. Not even a smart sailing ship in the present day, during a summer '*meltem*' or a norther of winter, blowing from the mountains of Crete [including Mount Ida itself], and with all its consequent squally or typhonic character, could fetch Phœnice without tacking five or six times at least. Many vessels would require three times as many tacks; and some would never reach it at all while such a wind lasted, but would be driven to the leeward of Clauda after vainly contending with heavy squalls in crossing Messara Bay, as St. Paul's ship was through being unable to beat up against the gale [to '*face the gale*,' in fact, not ' *bear up*,' as in our version], from its typhonic character."—Capt. Spratt's *Crete*, vol. ii. p. 17.—T. F.]

    [x]   " Barbaras Syrtes, ubi Maura semper
                  Æstuat unda."—*Horat. Carm.* ii. 6.
  " Inhospita Syrtes."—*Virgil.*
  " Semper naufraga Syrtis."—*Silius Italicus.*
  " Syrtibus hinc Libycis tuta est Ægyptus."—*Lucanus*, lib. viii. 444.
  [y] Shaw's *Travels*, p. 331.

supposition that the vessel went south. "Take it for granted that the Lesser Syrtis was meant, because it is more in a line with Malta; but, on the other hand, it is at a much greater distance than the Greater Syrtis; or, let us suppose it was either the Greater or the Lesser Syrtis—what are we to make of the word φοβούμενοι? How are we to reconcile their fears with their situation? They were under the island of Clauda; that is, 300 miles from the Greater Syrtis, and above 200 leagues from the Lesser Syrtis. The alarm was early, and the danger very remote. Writers make a wrong deduction. The word φοβούμενοι means only a remote apprehension from the uncertainty they were in : not any immediate fear. Had they been driven in the direction supposed, their fears would have increased in proportion as they approached the danger. They were continually approaching the danger if they advanced towards Malta. They are supposed to have been beating about these seas for fourteen days, yet nothing more is said respecting their fears of Syrtis, or of what the translation calls 'quick-sands.'" (B.) They get away from the island, and no more is said of Syrtis.—T. F.] [z]

---

[z] [It is said that the dread on the part of the sailors of being driven on Syrtis is conclusive that the wind was THEN northerly or north-easterly; and that as the island of Clauda was in sight, they could not have mistaken the direction of the wind. But the wind must have changed as they avoided Syrtis, and again changed to have reached either Malta or Meleda. As St. Paul's Bay is north of Malta, it must have changed again in order to have reached that bay—if that bay were seen. The wind is called "typhonic," and such a wind is variable. Mr. Smith proposed to add to the narrative that "storm sails" were set, and that thus the danger was averted!! Another unauthorised addition to the narrative might avoid the difficulty. *At the time* of the Voyage there were other dangers to apprehend than those of the sands of the Syrtes :—

> "Hoc tam segne solum raras tamen exerit herbas,
> Quos Nasamon gens dura legit, qui proxima ponto
> Nudus rura tenet, quem mundi barbara damnis
> Syrtis alit. Nam littoreis populator arenis
> Imminet, et nulla portus tangente carina,
> Novet opes. Sic cum toto commercia mundo
> Naufragiis Nasamones habent."—*Lucanus*, lib. ix. 438.

And this passage illustrates several inaccuracies of Ptolemy connected with the Mediterranean, or a change of territorial occupation between the time of the Voyage and the time when Ptolemy wrote. Strabo and Pliny place the Nasamones on the African coast near the Greater Syrtes, but

Ver 17. The storm still continuing, and probably from the same quarter, they lowered their sails, and were, it seems, according to the nautical expression, reduced to scud[a] under bare poles, and of course left nearly to the mercy and guidance of the elements.

Ver. 15. Both the Vulgate translation and Castalio render the words συναρπασθέντος τοῦ πλοίου by the word "correptus," a term of dubious signification, and not much explained either by our own or by the Rhemish version, both of which translate it by the word *caught*, by which it is rendered in most of the English versions. The Greek word is better explained in Schleusner, to mean "circumacta et agitata navi, procellarum vi, et ventorum impetu." [b]

Ver. 18. In this condition they seem to have been apprehensive, from the tossing of the vessel and her unmanageableness, that she Ver. 17.
Ver. 19. might founder or go to pieces: to prevent which, they bound it round under the keel or bottom with cables; an expedient alluded to by Horace,[c] and practised in later times.[d]

For the same purpose of preservation they lightened the ship, and on the third day made a further sacrifice by casting

---

Ptolemy places them in the inland region of Augila. [*Dict. of G. and R. Geography* vox "Nasamones."] Ptolemy must also have erred, when opposed to other authorities, in placing his names of the border seas of the Mediterranean. He seems to have certainly erred as respects the Adriatic Gulf itself in the use of the word "Ionian" as applied to the coast of Apulia.—T. F.]

[a] [Mr. Smith (p. 105, and see p. 98) says, "Rightly rendered by Canon Wordsworth, 'We gave the ship to the gale and *scudded* before it.' But 'when a ship, *steering* for a port, is drifted by a current, it is evident that, unless it be exactly with her, or exactly against her, it will throw her out of her intended course.' "—Raper on *Navigation*, 5th ed. p. 91. But this ship was drifting and not steering, and, according to Mr. Smith, it drifted in almost a straight line from Clauda to the northern side of the island of Malta. It had certainly no current to favour this direction, even if it had been steered.—T. F.]

[b] Dr. Hammond's paraphrase approaches nearly to the interpretation of Schleusner: "And the ship being carried by force along with it (the wind Euroclydon), and being not able to resist or hold up against the wind, letting her loose, we were carried," &c.

[c]   ". . . ac sine funibus
       Vix durare carinæ
       Possint imperiosius
          Æquor?"—*Hor. Carm.* i. 14.

[d] See Anson's *Voyage.*

out the tackling or furniture ᵉ of the ship. But the storm not abating, they gave up all hopes of safety,ᶠ as they were totally ignorant of their situation, and conscious only that they were at the mercy of the winds and waves. They continued fourteen days in this state of anxiety, but at length discovered that they were driven into the Adriatic Sea, perhaps from some abatement of the gloom, and some knowledge of the coast at its entrance, where it is narrowest.

ᵉ [The Very Rev. Dean Alford adopted the word "furniture." The Latin equivalent would probably be the word "armamenta," used by Suetonius (*ante*, p. 11).—T. F.]

ᶠ [Mr. Smith, without any reverence for the words of St. Luke, added to the difficulties of the voyage, and endeavoured to enlarge the narrative by the aid of pure fiction, unconnected by any probability with expressed words. He asks (p. 115), "Why their hope of being saved had been taken away?" "The *true* explanation," he replies, "I apprehend is this: their exertions to subdue *the leak* (!) had been unavailing; they could not tell which way to make for the nearest land in order to run their ship ashore, the only resource for a *sinking* (!) ship; but unless they did land they must founder at sea."

"Their apprehensions, *therefore*, were not so much caused by the fury of the tempest *as by the state of the ship!*" These facts of the Voyage have been hitherto unknown, and the "sinking" ship did not sink.—T. F.]

THE THEORY OF MR. SMITH.

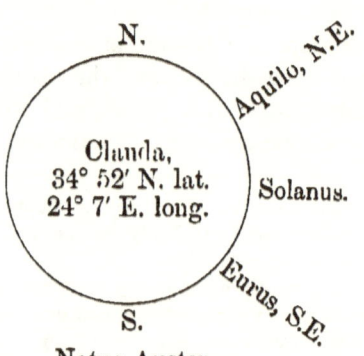

Malta [Koura Point],
35° 56′ N. lat.

O————————

Distance, 477 miles.

The sea current is east-
ward and southward
at Malta.

[Malta is 1° 4′ north of Clauda. According to Mr. Smith,
the mean direction of the wind from Clauda was E. 26° 15′ N.,
or about E.N.E. ½° N. and the following was his theory :—

1. That the wind which blew was a "point wind," that is a
wind blowing steadily from one point,—*for I consider that no
change took place in its direction during the remainder of the
voyage.*" (Page 101.)

2. That the vessel drifted 36½ miles in twenty-four hours.
(Page 123.)

3. That the vessel did not go south, for the wind which drove
them "when yielding to it" to Clauda would, "if they had continued to scud, have driven them *directly* to Syrtis." (Page 101.)
Not if the wind went southerly or was changeable.

4. That they turned the ship's head off shore, and *set such
sail* as the violence of the gale would permit them to carry.
"We may be certain this was the course adopted,—*though the
historian is silent.*" (Page 109.)

5. That the ship was laid on the starboard tack under the
lee of Clauda, as only on this tack could they avoid the African
coast. (Page 109.)

They had struck sail, and were driven, the ship apparently
having become unmanageable [verse 17]: but Mr. Smith
affected to know better than this, and he therefore affirmed

they would have been wrecked "had the ship been allowed to be driven at the mercy of the winds, *as is generally supposed.*" (Page 112.)

6. "Strake sail and so were driven" means, Mr. Smith said, "they were thus borne along" undergirded, made snug, *with storm sails set*, and on the starboard tack, with the wind E.N.E. This, he said, was the only course to avoid Syrtis, and thus ended the first day (p. 113). But Captain Spratt says ('Crete,' vol. ii. p. 19), "Had the gale been E.N.E., there would not have been a necessity to face it: with easy sail and little leeway a Chinese junk would have fetched Phœnice; and even, almost without any sail set, she would have drifted towards the port." Thus this theory is disposed of by the highest authority.

7. On the second day they lightened the ship [verse 18]; on the third day they cast out the tackling of the ship [verse 19]; and in "many days" [verse 20], that is, *some* or *several* of the fourteen days, neither sun nor stars appeared, and "no small tempest lay on us." They were at the mercy of the winds.

Paul Hoste remarked [*Smith*, p. 208] "that no person could infer, *à priori*, that a vessel impelled by the wind could sail to a place which, in respect to that from which it started, was directly to the windward." This objection is well stated,— namely, "the vessel—the sail-less hulk simply—impelled by the wind." The reply of Mr. Smith is, "This may be true; but, on the other hand, no person who tried to impel a vessel *by sails* could avoid making the discovery; for, on the most unfavourable supposition—that *of a sail* set at right angles to the keel—it would be discovered, that even though the wind did not blow directly upon it—*so long as the sail was full*— the vessel would go ahead; and, of course, *if the yard could be braced*, she would go nearer to the wind than at right angles to it, or within eight points." On this the following note has been made:—"Who Paul Hoste may be I know not. But his remark is very true. The paradox can only be explained by those who know the peculiar action of keels and lee-boards. Without some such appliances no sailing ship could get to the windward. The reply of Mr. Smith is idiotic."

If the suggested demonstration in answer to Paul Hoste needs a reference to the use of *sails*, not merely is Paul Hoste unanswered, but he is unanswerable.

D

8. Then we get a drifting theory :

The distance from Clauda to Koura Point, Malta, or to St. Paul's Bay, is 477 miles. At page 125 Mr. Smith gives a common calculation for this distance, and produces the result as something remarkable. The case he solves is a very simple one ; it is this: "Given the differences of the longitude and of the latitude of two places, to find the course and distance." The difference of latitude gives the length of one side of a right-angled triangle, and the difference of longitude gives the length of another side ; then the angle of the course sought is a fixed result, and is independent of winds, though this might not be inferred from the form of the statement in the book. Then, having the length of the sides of a right-angled triangle and one of the other angles, the length of the hypothenuse, or the distance it represents, is ascertained: or, in this case, 476 or 477 miles. This is obviously and necessarily a fixed distance existing at all times ; but the inference it presents to our notice contradicts the argument of Mr. Smith. The distance from point to point being 477 miles in a straight line, is it to be believed or can it with any probability of truth be affirmed, that the storm, which on some days was so severe as to cause darkness, drifted the ship day by day, as Mr. Smith says it did [p. 124], at an even rate, without sails, of $36\frac{1}{2}$ miles per day, from point to point,—that the wind blew equally strong the whole distance—that the wind was always the same " without any change in its direction," though they " were tossed about,"—and that the force of the eastward set of the current off Malta is to be disregarded ?

The recorded change of the effect of the wind must have caused changes in the position of the vessel far from a straight course to Malta, and also changes in the rate of drifting. The narrative itself shows that there was increasing and diminishing severity in the storm, and, therefore, a very variable course of sailing. The rate of drifting is utterly unascertainable. Taking the distance from Clauda to Meleda at 630 miles [p. 170], and allowing forty-five miles a day for the set of the current in Adria, and for a storm drifting them to the north, and being " tossed about " in the dark tempest during many of the days, a similar calculation would bring the ship to Meleda in fourteen days ; but, in fact, any such estimates are worthless.

Admiral Penrose, an advocate of this drift theory, so little understood the question, that he decided it—making a mistake of 150 miles—before he knew where Meleda was, and excused his ignorance of the position of the island because he had not seen Bryant's work. It was thought his mistake was "immaterial to his argument!" It was not immaterial as regarded the judicial impressibility of his mind. (*Smith,* 170, 26.)

9. The theory of Dr. Falconer and other writers is a very reasonable one. He said : " I find from ancient writers that at the time of the year when the storm arose there was usually tempestuous weather : variable and southerly winds. If such usual winds blew at the time of the voyage, the vessel would have been driven towards the north." Then as regards Malta it is asked : " Do the words of Cicero and of Diodorus Siculus, in reference to the island of Malta, create such an impression on the mind that the account they give of the island, and the account given by St. Luke of that island where the shipwreck happened, refer to the same island ? " It will, also, be shown by the evidence of ALL contemporary writers, hereafter cited, who name the limits of the sea of Adria, that they do not place Malta in the Adriatic but in the African sea, and that they do not call the expanse of sea between Sicily and Greece, or Crete and Malta, the Adriatic. In order to assist in forming a correct conclusion, the concurrent opinions of ancient and contemporary geographers on the locality of Melite and their definition of the word "Adria" are cited. We may come to a conclusion one way or another; we may say the evidence preponderates on the side of Meleda and not on that of Malta : but the reader may claim to know correctly why differences of opinion prevail.—T. F.]

ADRIA.

" When the fourteenth night was come, as we were driven up and down in ADRIA [διαφερομένων ἡμῶν ἐν τῷ Ἀδρίᾳ— driven along in or through Adria], about midnight the sailors deemed that they drew near to some country " [οἱ ναῦται προσανέχειν τινὰ αὐτοῖς χώραν : — that some country drew near to them].

It may be necessary in this place to give some account of the boundaries or limits of the Adriatic Sea.[g] These are to be inferred from writers of the best contemporary authority, not from casual or ambiguous expressions of later or of inferior geographers. [" We ought," says Mr. Bryant, " to inquire of what rank and of what age the writers are whose authority is appealed to. It is not sufficient to be told what is said, unless we are likewise informed when and by whom it was delivered.

---

[g] " [The sea that bounded the western coast of Italy bore the several names of Mare Inferum, Tyrrhenum et Etruscum; while those of Mare Superum, Hadriaticum, or Hadriacum, were attached to the Eastern or Adriatic Sea. The latter wa sknown to the Greeks by the name of Ἀδρίας (Herod. i. 163) or Ἰόνιος κόλπος (Thuc. i. 24), but they seem to have understood by the name of ' Ionium Mare ' that portion of it which lies between the south of Italy taken from the Iapygian promontory and the Peloponnesus. The narrow strait which separates the extremity of Italy from Sicily, received its appellation from that island; but it was not confined to this arm alone, since we find the name of ' Mare Siculum ' applied to the waters which washed the western coast of Greece." (Strab. ii. 123; Plin. iv. 5.)—Cramer's Ancient Italy, i. 3.

" The name ' Ionian Gulf ' appears, says M. Gosselin, to have extended from the Acroceraunian mountains to the southern part of Dalmatia, near Lissus, now Alessio, to the bottom of the Gulf of Drin."— Strabo, vii. 5, § 9; translation, p. 486. (41° 37′ N. lat., 19° 2°′ E. long.) " The Promontorium Iapygium or Sallentinum presented a conspicuous landmark to mariners sailing from Greece to Sicily; the fleets of Athens, after passing the Peloponnesus, on this passage, making for Corcyra, from whence they steered straight across to the Promontorium Iapygium (Capo di Leuca), coasting along the south of Italy for the rest of the voyage."—Strabo (translation), vol. i. p. 428, n. If the ' Castor and Pollux ' was on this course, she might easily have sailed to Meleda in the Adriatic.

Bochart says that Malta lies in the line that all ships went that sailed to Italy. In this he was undoubtedly in error. Bryant, in reply, remarked that the words εἰς νῆσον δέ τινα ἡμᾶς δεῖ ἐκπεσεῖν mean " the island we shall be cast on is out of our true course or direction." Lucian, also, says Bryant, describes the usual course of sailing in his Dialogue Πλοῖον ἢ Εὐχαί. A ship set sail from the Nile with a brisk gale, and on the seventh day had got as far as Acamas, the western promontory of Cyprus. Then the wind came full against them, and they were obliged to run obliquely up to Sidon. From thence they shaped the very same course as the ship of St. Paul running under the coast of Pamphylia where they were nearly lost on the Chelidonian rocks. Then they coasted Lycia and got as high as Cnidus, but whereas the apostle's ship turned off to the left to get shelter by Crete, this ship, finding it had lost its voyage, stood across the Ægean Sea for Attica, and after much difficulty came to anchor in the Piræus. This was effected in seventy days after they had sailed from the Pharos, when it was said they ought to have been at the mouth of the Tiber.—T. F.]

We must make use of the lines we are treating of as a standard, and not be guided by the mistakes and extravagances of after ages. The only way to arrive at the truth is to learn the sentiments of the best authors who lived in or near to the times we are engaged in, and observe how things were defined and specified when the apostle wrote. I shall not descend for evidence to the fourth, fifth, or any lower centuries, but confine myself to the testimony of writers who were either, therefore, contemporaries, or not many years antecedent or subsequent to the Apostolic age."—B.]

[They were in Adria at *the end* of the Voyage. Until the end of the Voyage Adria is not mentioned. They were in Adria on the fourteenth morning, and probably earlier. The sea in which a ship comes into port or is wrecked is a fact in respect of which it might be presumed there could be no equivocation, doubt, or controversy. When a sea is named, it may be inferred that the common well-known name is used, because writing down a name is an act of deliberation and intended to convey accurate information to those whose common knowledge would recognise the place indicated by the name given to it.

There were two islands anciently named Melita: one sometimes called "Melita Africana," and now called MALTA:—the other, sometimes called "Melita Illyrica," and now called MELEDA, on the Illyrian coast, not far from Ragusa and north of the city of Dyrrachium, now called Durazzo.

If "*Melita Africana*," or "MALTA," was known about the year A.D. 60 to be in part of the Mediterranean Sea, then designated or known as "Adria," then "Malta," it may be inferred, was the scene of the shipwreck. If all contemporary authors, beyond dispute, place "*Melita Illyrica*" only, and not "*Melita Africana*," in "Adria," then they determine the fact that the island now called "MELEDA" was the actual scene of that event. There is no doubt whatever that *Melita Illyrica*, or "MELEDA," was in "*Adria*," and this has necessarily been conceded by all writers. Was Malta in "ADRIA"? The use of the name "Adria" by those who wrote long after the Voyage, almost ages after it [for such are cited], can be of no importance in opposition to writers who, at the time of the Voyage, had abundance of opportunity to use the name correctly, and who cannot be presumed to have used the name in a different sense from its use by all other known writers who lived when they were living. If, being contemporaneous and independent authorities, they all concur in a meaning they distinctly give to the word "Adria," then we may be assured they truthfully instruct us unless some probability of error can be suggested. As respects personal facts, there may always be the possibility of mistake or misrepresentation. As respects the names of seas or places, it is in the highest degree improbable that many persons living at the same time can have been mistaken in nominating them when there is a common agreement in their writings designating such seas or places by the same names. The affirmation of Mr. Smith is made in these words : —"Was the sea which is interposed between CRETE AND MALTA termed 'Adria' when the narrative was written?" Mr. Smith replied by saying "This sea, as well as the gulf at present known by the same name, was then known as the 'Adriatic.' The proof of this is very easily established. Ptolemy, who flourished *immediately* after St. Luke, describes this sea so often and so *particularly by this name* as to leave the point *without a shadow of doubt.*" (Smith, pp. 158-159.) (Ptolemy was alive in A.D. 160.)

Then, again (p. 162), Mr. Smith says, "that the date of the narrative of the Voyage was about A.D. 63," and that, "in point of fact, there is ample evidence that this name [Adria] was given to the lower sea between CRETE and MALTA before either Ptolemy or Pausanias wrote." (Smith, pp. 162, 163.)

In the last Essay on the subject (" Life of St. Paul," by the Very Rev. Dr. Howson, the Dean of Chester, vol. ii. p. 427), it is said (the words I assume to be those of the late Mr. Smith), "Not only do the Classical Poets use the name of 'Adria' for *all* the natural division of the Mediterranean which lies between SICILY and GREECE, but the same phraseology is to be found in the Historians and Geographers." The words used by Mr. Smith in his own book, p. 158, are "between CRETE and MALTA," and not the words " between *Sicily and Greece.*" The difference of expression apparently may have arisen from the remembrance of the fact that the writers alluded to placed Malta in the African sea ! It would have been a proper caution to have pointed this fact out to the notice of readers. If poets, historians, and geographers so unanimously agreed, it is to be regretted no pains were taken to name them in the argument. That we have not been favoured with a citation of the important passages from their writings which would have thus accurately presented to us their "phraseology" free from all doubt and have made their evidence clear is significant of the difficulty of finding such phraseology. Why, for instance, have cited writers who lived at so remote a period after the Voyage as Ptolemy (A.D. 160) and Pausanias (A.D. 174), when Historians and Geographers of an earlier date are so distinctly referred to, though not named and the two who are named are not (as will be presently shown) authorities, for the inference it is intended the reader should draw? Let us, however, first cite all writers who can aid us living while St. Luke and St. Paul were alive.—T. F.]

POMPONIUS MELA.

[Pomponius Mela, who lived about the years A.D. 41–54, was the first Roman author who composed a formal treatise upon Geography (*Dict. of G. and R. Biography*, vol. ii. p. 1011), and it is said to be highly probable that he flourished under the Emperor Claudius (A.D. 41–54). It is perfectly clear that he most distinctly excludes Malta from the sea of Adria, and he also connects Malta with Africa. The information he purported to give embodied the names of territories, seas, and localities known at the time he was writing, and it must have appeared as absurd and erroneous in his day to have said that Malta was in the Adriatic as it would be to say the same at the present time.

"Mare quod primo sinu accipit, Ægæum dicitur: quod sequenti, in ore, IONIUM; ADRIATICUM *interius:* quod ultimo nos *Thuscum,* Graii *Tyrrhenum* perhibent. Gentium prima est Scythia, alia quam dicta est, a Tanai in media fermè Pontici lateris; hinc in Ægæi partem pertinens Thracia. Huic Macedonia adjungitur. Tum Græcia prominet, *Ægæumque ab Ionio mari dirimit.* ADRIATICI latus Illyris occupat. Inter ipsum ADRIATICUM *et Thuscum* Italia procurrit." (Lib. i. ch. 3, l. 15, p. 27; ed. Lug. Bat. 1772.)

(44)

"In Epiro nihil Ambarcio sinu nobilius est.[h] Facit sinus, qui angustis faucibus et quæ minus mille passibus pateant, grande pelagus admittit. Faciunt urbes quæ assidunt; Actium, Argia, Amphilochis, Ambracia, Æacidarum regna Pyrrhique. Buthroton ultra est. *Deinde Ceraunii montes :* AB IIS *flexus* IN ADRIAM. Hoc mare magno recessu litorum acceptum et vaste quidem in latitudinem patens qua penetrat tamen vastius, Illyricis usque Tergeste, cetera Gallicis Italicisque gentibus cingitur; Parthini et Dassaretæ prima ejus tenent: sequentia Taulantii, Euchelico, Phæaces. Deinde sunt, quos proprie Illyricos vocant. Tum Pyræi et Liburni et Istria. Urbium prima est Oricum, secunda Dyrrachium, Epidamnos ante erat. Romani nomen mutavere quia velut in damnum ituris, omen id visum est." (Lib. ii. ch. 3, l. 140, p. 170.)

"Contra Ambracium sinum, Leucadia, et vicina ADRIATICO MARI, Corcyra." (Lib. ii. ch. 6, l. 90, p. 217.)

"Circa Siciliam, in *Siculo freto* est Æœe, quam Calypso habitasse dicitur; AFRICAM versus Gaulos, MELITA, Cosura," &c. (Lib. ii. ch. 7, l. 160, p. 224.)—T. F.]

---

[h] "A view of this fine basin cannot fail to suggest the idea of a naval and commercial station of the first order; it was such in antiquity, and its natural conditions are the same as ever; its central position, its teeming fisheries, extensive salines, the plain of Arta, the encircling mountains clothed with forests; these and many other advantages are so many appeals to human industry and enterprise—it is not in the nature of things that such appeals should for ever be unheeded."—*Stuart on Epirus,* Geo. Soc. Jour. 1869, p. 283.

"Epirus has never recovered from the desolating chastisement inflicted on it by Æmilius Paulus 167 years B.C.; and at this day the country with its fine climate, its varied resources, and commanding position, is appealing to man to recommence the work of scientific industry and progressive improvement."—*Stuart on Epirus,* p. 296.

"Such is Macedonia, which was once the mistress of the world, which extended her career over Asia, Armenia, Iberia, Albania, Cappadocia, Syria, Egypt, Taurus, and Caucasus; which reduced the whole of the East under her power, and triumphed over the Bactri, the Medes, and the Persians. She, too, it was who proved the conqueror of India, thus treading in the footsteps of Father Liber and of Hercules; and this is the same Macedonia, of which our own general, Æmilius Paulus, sold to pillage seventy-two cities in one day. So great is the difference of her lot, resulting from the actions of two men."—*Pliny.*

STRABO.

[He was born about B.C. 66, at Amasia, now "*Jekil Irmak*." In the year B.C. 24 he was at Syene, in Egypt. He was well-informed respecting the Adriatic and had visited Rome.

He says :—" The remainder of Italy is long and narrow and terminates in two promontories, one extending to the strait of Sicily, the other to Iapygia [Capo di Leuca, 39° 47′ N. lat., and 18° 22′ E. long.] It is embraced, *on one side* by the Adriatic, on the other by the Tyrrhenian Sea. The form and size of the Adriatic resembles that portion of Italy bounded by the Apennines and the two seas, and extending as far as Iapygia and the isthmus which separates the Gulf of Taranto from that of Posidonium " (*Salerno*, 40° 40′ N. lat., and 14° 15′ E. long.)—*Strabo*, lib. v. ch. 1, sec. 3; translation, vol. i. p. 315.

" Here is the Temple of Minerva, which formerly was rich, and the rock called Iapygia which juts out far into the sea towards the rising of the sun in winter and turning, as it were, towards Cape Lacinium, which lies opposite to it on the west, it closes the entrance of the Gulf of Tarentum, as, on the other side, the Ceraunian mountains, together with the said Cape, *close the entrance of the Ionian Gulf.*" (Lib. vi. ch. 3, sec. 5; translation, vol. i. p. 428-429.)

" Next to Apollonia is Bylliace and Oricum, with its naval arsenal Panormus and the Ceraunian mountains, *which form the commencement of the entrance of the* IONIAN AND ADRIATIC GULFS (τοῦ Ἰονίου κόλπου καὶ τοῦ Ἀδρίου). The mouth is common to both : but this difference is to be observed, that the name 'Ionian' is applied to the first part of the Gulf only, and 'Adriatic' to the interior sea up to the farthest end; but the name 'Adriatic' is now applied to the whole sea."[1]— *Strabo*, vii. 7, sec. 9; W. Falconer's translation, vol. i. p. 486.

Strabo also represents part of the coast of Epirus to have been washed by the *Sicilian* Sea. " From Apollonia to Macedonia is the Egnatian way : its direction is towards the

---

[1] Admiral Smyth misunderstood this explanation, and inferred that the name included the IONIAN Sea.

east, and the distance is measured by pillars at every mile as far as Cypselus and the river Hebrus. The first part of it is called the road to Candavia, which is an Illyrian mountain. It passes through Lychnidus, a city, and Pylon, a place which separates Illyria from Macedonia. Thence its direction is beside Barnus, &c., and Pella, as far as *Thessalonica*." (Lib. vii. ch. 7, sec. 4.) " The course for passengers from Greece and Asia is most direct to Brundusium, and, in fact, all who are journeying to Rome disembark here." (Lib. vi. ch. 3, sec. 7.) Cicero, on being exiled, went to Brundusium, and, after staying there thirteen days, crossed the sea and landed at Dyrrachium. On his road through Macedonia he was met by his friend Plancius, quæstor in Macedonia, who took him to his official residence in Thessalonica, where they arrived the 23rd of May, B.C. 58. (See Long's accurate and able *History of the Decline of the Roman Empire*, vol. iii. p. 458.) When Cicero returned to Rome from Thessalonica, he left Dyrrachium on the 4th, and arrived at Brundusium on the 5th of August, B.C. 57. Roman armies had often crossed the Adriatic from Brindisi and a knowledge of what was called the " Adriatic " must have been general at Rome. —T. F.]

MARCUS ANNÆUS LUCANUS.

[He died A.D. 65, at the time when, in fact, St. Paul was at Rome. He calls the expanse of the Mediterranean " The Ionian Sea."

" Sonat in Ionio vagus Adria ponto." (Lib. v. 613.)

Dyrrachium.[k]

" Non opus hanc veterum, nec moles structa tuetur,
Humanusque labor, facilis, licet ardua tollat,
Cedere vel bellis, vel cuncta moventibus annis,
Sed munimen habet nullo quassabile ferro,

---

[k] Cæsar (*Bell. Civ.* lib. iii. ch. 26) relates a remarkable escape of a vessel from capture through a sudden change of wind from south to south-west, after a chase past Dyrrachium, the south wind having blown for two days. (See *Lucanus*, lib. v. 605, &c.) And stormy weather delayed Cæsar at Brundusium (Brindisi) during the month of December (*Appiani de Bellis Civil.* lib. ii. ch. 16, p. 757; Amstelod. Jansson, 1670).

Naturam sedemque loci, nam clausa profundo
Undique præcipiti, scopulisque vomentibus æquor,
Exiguo debet, quod non est insula, colli.
Terribiles ratibus sustentant mœnia cautes,
IONIUMQUE furens, rapido cum tollitur Austro,
Templa, domosque quatit, spumatque in culmina pontus."

Lucanus, lib. vi. 19.

Brundusium.

" Urbs est Dictæis olim possessa colonis,
Quos *Creta* profugos vexere per æquora puppes
Cecropiæ, victum mentitis *Thesea* velis.
Hanc latus angustum jam se cogentis in arctum
Hesperiæ, tenuem producit in æquora linguam,
ADRIACAS flexis caudit quæ cornibus undas.
Nec tamen hoc arctis immissum faucibus æquor
Portus erat, si non violentos insula Coros
Exciperet saxis, lassasque refunderet undas.
Hinc illinc moles scopulosæ rupis aperto
Opposuit natura mari, flatusque removit,
Et tremulo starent contentæ funo carinæ.
Hinc late patet omne fretum seu vela ferantur
In portus *Corcyra* tuos, seu læva petatur.
Illyris Ionias vergens EPIDAMNUS [*Dyrrachium*] in undas.
Huc fuga nautarum, cum totas ADRIA vires
Movit, et in nubes abiere *Ceraunia*, cumque
Spumoso Calaber perfunditur æquore Sason." [*Sassa.*]

Lucanus, lib. ii. 610.

Æas.

" Ergo abrupta palus multos discessit in amnes
Purus in occasus, parvi sed gurgitis *Æas*
Ionio fluit inde mari."—*Lucanus*, lib. vi. 361.

The river Æas [now *Viosa* or *Vovussa*] ran through the pass
named " Fauces Antigonenses," now the *Stena* of the *Viosa*, and
joined the sea a little above Apollonia, not far from Aulon, or
Avlona.

It was the Ionian Sea, driven by the raging south-wind,
which shook the foundations of Dyrrachium : it was to Brindisi
the sailor fled when the storm in Adria was violent, when Acroceraunia was hid in the clouds, and the island of Sassa was
enveloped in the foam of the ocean, and it was into the Ionian
Sea the river Æas discharged itself. This description defines
the limits of Adria.—T. F.]

C. PLINIUS.

[Pliny was born A.D. 23, and died A.D. 79, and was, therefore, about thirty-seven years old when the Voyage occurred.

His testimony is of peculiar importance. The voyage of St. Paul was in the year A.D. 60. · Pliny must have been at Rome while St. Paul was there: he must have been acquainted with seas and ships, for he had been appointed admiral by Vespasian, and in the year A.D. 79 he was stationed with the fleet at Misenum when the great eruption of Vesuvius (opposite to Puteoli) occurred, which overwhelmed Herculaneum and Pompeii, and caused his own death.

Defining the names of the seas of the Great Gulf, he says, "The sea from which this gulf takes its rise is called the '*Atlantic*;' by some the '*Great Atlantic*;' the entrance of which is, by the Greeks, called '*Porthmos*,' by us, 'the *Straits of Gades*.' After its entrance, as far as it washes the coast of Spain, it is called the '*Hispanian Sea*,' though some give to it the name of the '*Iberian or Balearic Sea*.' Where it faces the province of Gallia Narbonensis it has the name of the '*Gallic*,' and, after that, of the '*Ligurian Sea*.' From Liguria to the island of Sicily it is called the '*Tuscan Sea*,'—the same sea which is called by some of the Greeks the '*Notian*,' by others the '*Tyrrhenian*,' while many of our people call it the '*Lower Sea*.' Beyond Sicily, as far as the country of the Salentini (Calabria), it is called by Polybius the '*Ausonian Sea*.' Eratosthenes, however, gives to the whole expanse that lies between the inlet of the Ocean and the island of Sardinia the name of the '*Sardoan Sea*;' thence to Sicily, the '*Tyrrhenian*;' thence to Crete, the '*Sicilian*;' and, beyond that island, the '*Cretan Sea*.'"

Thus, the ancient authorities referred to by Pliny do not name "Adria" as applied to the sea south of Italy. (*Plinius*, Lug. Bat. 1669, lib. iii. ch. 8, pp. 151, 152; Riley's translation, vol. i. pp. 210, 222.)

Then, again: "At Accra Iapygia, Italy projects the greatest distance into the sea. At nineteen miles from this point is the town of Basta (Vaste near Poggiordo), and then Hydruntum (Otranto), *where the 'Ionian' is separated from the 'Adriatic Sea*,'

and from which the distance, across to Greece, is the shortest."
(Lib. iii. ch. 11, p. 162; translation, p. 226.) "In this gulf, as
we have distinguished the limits, are two seas: the Ionian in
the first part, and the inner the Adriatic, which is called the
Upper Sea":—"In eo duo maria quo distinximus fine, Ionium
in prima parte, interius Hadriaticum quod Superum vocant."
(Lib. iii. ch. 26, p. 265.)

And Pliny removed all doubt of what he believed to be the
limits of the Adriatic when he wrote, "Byzantium (Constan-
tinople), a free State, formerly called 'Lygos,' distant from
Dyrrachium 711 miles, so great being the space (longitudo) of
land between the Adriatic Sea and the Propontis." (Lib. iv.
ch. 11, p. 207; translation, p. 307.)

He further says, "Mox Leucothia, extraque conspectum,
PELAGUS AFRICANUM attingens, Sardinia." (Lib. iii. ch. 6, p.
155.) "Insulæ sunt in AFRICAM versæ Gaulos, MELITA a
Camerina . . . Cosyra," &c. (Lib. iii. ch. 8, p. 159.) Thus he
placed Malta in the African Sea, while he placed the Ionian
Sea south of the Adriatic Sea.

Pliny further removes all connection, by name, between Adria
and the southern sea, in saying, "Many are the gulfs which
penetrate the shores of the Peloponnesus, and many the seas
which roar around it. Invaded by the 'Ionian' on the north,
it is beaten by the 'Sicilian' on the west, buffeted by the
'Cretan' on the south, by the 'Ægean' on the S.E., and by
the 'Myrtoan' on the N.E., which last sea begins at the Gulf of
Megara, and washes all the coast of Attica." (Lib. iv. ch. 5,
p. 196; trans. p. 285.) And he mentions that "the Greeks divide
the Ionian Sea into the 'Sicilian' and the 'Cretan' seas, after
the names of those islands, and they give the name 'Icarian' to
that part which lies between Samos and Myconos." (Lib. iv.
ch. 11, p. 210; trans. p. 309.) The seas thus named separated
Adria from the African sea, and, therefore, no island in the
African sea could have been in Adria while intermediate seas
retained distinct names: and the Adriatic did not include the
Ionian, the Sicilian, or the Cretan seas.

Pliny names both the islands called Melite. Of the Dalmatian or Illyrian Melite he relates, "That at a distance of twenty
miles from Issa is Corcyra (Curzola), called Melæna, with a
town founded by the Cnidians; between which and Illyricum is

MELITA (Meleda), from whence come, as we learn from Callima-
chus, certain little dogs called 'Melitæi.'" (Lib. iii. ch. 26,
p. 186; trans. p. 267.) Pliny names the islands of Gaulos (Gozzo)
near Malta and Galata (Calata) thus, "Mox Gaulos et Gelata
cujus terra scorpiones, dirum animal Africæ, necat"—" The soil
kills the scorpion." (Lib. v. ch. 7; Teubner's edition, vol. i.
p. 191.) These islands Pliny, as well as Strabo and Ptolemy,
included in the AFRICAN sea: "sunt insulæ in Africam versæ
Gaulos, Melita," &c. (Lib. iii. ch. 8 [14]; Teubner's ed. p. 141.)
—T. F.]

On Pliny's statements Mr. Bryant (p. 378) makes these remarks. "Pliny, speaking of Hydruntum, at the bottom of the
Gulf, says, it was 'the boundary of the forementioned seas' —
'Hydruntum ad discrimen Ionii et Adriatici maris;' not
'discrimen *inter se*,' to distinguish one from the other, as
Harduin fondly imagines. No limit or mark can distinguish
two places both on the same side, but it was the boundary
which separated them from the seas below; from the Tarentine
and Epirotic, the Sicilian and Cretan seas; which last con-
stituted the great 'Ionian.' But Pliny seldom takes notice of
it by that name; though he allows that the Greeks called it
so: '*Græci Ionium dividunt in Siculum ac Creticum ab insulis.*
Harduin was misled by Pliny's calling it the '*Ionian Sea*,'
and not the '*Ionian Gulf*.' But we must observe it was seldom
called '*Sinus Ionius*,' or 'Ἰόνιος κόλπος, but by writers who
supposed it to comprehend the whole gulf, such as Thucydides
[B.C. 423], Theophrastus [B.C. 322], Appian [A.D. 140], Herodian
[A.D. 238], Dio Cassius [A.D. 180]. When it is divided into
two seas, according to Polybius [B.C. 167], Diodorus [B.C. 8],
and Pliny [A.D. 67], it is then denominated 'Ἰόνιος πόρος and
'*Ionium Mare*.' Yet, under whatever name it comes, it must
never be confounded with the great 'Ionian.' That began at
Tænarus and the Strophades [*Insulæ Ionio in magno*], and comprehended, as I before mentioned, the 'Cretan and Sicilian'
seas—which Pliny takes proper notice of—*Græci Ionium dividunt in Siculum ac Creticum ab insulis.* (Lib. iv. ch. 11.)
In respect to the Upper Ionian, Strabo intimates that it was
properly called 'Ἰόνιος κόλπος, as originally possessing the whole
sinus, but that in his time it was esteemed but as a part of the
Adriatic; nay, the Adriatic had, in a manner, engrossed the

whole. As to the notion of Bochart that the 'Sinus' and 'Mare Adriaticum' were distinguished from each other—the one being within the 'Sinus' and the other far without—it is a groundless supposition; nor is there the least shadow of authority for such an opinion in any author from Herodotus to Pliny."—B.

DIODORUS SICULUS.

[He was born in Sicily, and it is said to be highly probable he wrote his great work after the year B.C. 8. His place is within the early years of the Christian era. He called the sea between Carthage and Panormus (Palermo), that is, the sea south of Italy, the "*Libyan Sea*" (book ii. ch. 2), and the expanse of sea to the east of Sicily "The Ionian." " Dionysius, tyrant of Syracuse," he wrote, " determined to establish cities in Adria for the purpose of having in his power the passage called ' *Ionian*,' so that he might be secure in crossing to Epirus, and have cities of his own as stations for his ships." (Book xv. ch. 13.)

We have, therefore, his authority for limits of the Mediterranean Sea by his use of names, which exclude Malta from the Adriatic Sea. The "Ionian passage," said Mr. Bryant, was so called, " because the Roman armies as well as private persons passed from Brundusium to Epidamnus, and to the opposite continent." The sea, therefore, south of the Ionian passage, could not have been even popularly known as the Adriatic, for the sea north of this passage was Adria, and at Rome this must have been well known, and, also, at Thessalonica in Macedonia. —T. F.]

LUCIUS ANNÆUS SENECA.

[He died A.D. 65, and was very probably in Rome at the time St. Paul arrived there. He wrote :—

"Hadriam, et Ionium Ægeumque."—*Epist.* 1, lib. xiv.

The Adriatic, the Ionian, and the Egean, are names which preclude Malta from having been regarded by him to have been in the Adriatic. The following verses afford the same conclusion :—

        . . . " quæ ferarum immanitas,
    Quæ Scylla, quæ Charybdis, *Ausonium* mare
    Siculumque sorbens, quæque anhelantem premens
    Titana tantis Ætna fervescit minis ? "—*Medea,* act iii. 408.

Again :—

        " Non Eurus rapiens mare,
        Aut sævus rabidus freto
        Ventosi tumor Adriæ,
        Quem non lancea militis,
        Non strictus domuit chalybs " [*gladius è Chalybe*].
                Thyestes, act ii. 362, edit. Amstel. 1662.

To this passage Thomas Farnabius adds this remark:—
" Maris Adriatici procellis obnoxii, utpote ventis, maxime Noto
expositi."—T. F.]

FLAVIUS JOSEPHUS.

[He was born at Jerusalem A.D. 37, and died A.D. 93. He
says that Pompey fled beyond the "*Ionian* Sea" (Hist. book i.
ch. 9, sec. 1), and that when he (Josephus) was on his way to
Rome, the vessel foundered in the Adriatic. (Life, ch. 3,
sec. 2.) Therefore, according to this writer, the Ionian Sea was
distinguished from the Adriatic. This obvious inference is an
answer to the cool statement of Mr. Smith (p. 168) that the shipwreck of Josephus could not have happened in the Gulf!"—T. F.]

ARISTARCHUS,
THE MACEDONIAN OF THESSALONICA.

[We are clearly entitled to place the companions of St. Paul
among those who had an accurate knowledge of the general
limits of the sea as popularly known, or called by contemporary
writers, by the name of "Adria." His means of knowledge
are indicated by his being described as of Thessalonica, a city
at the eastern termination of the great Egnatian Way, from
the city of Dyrrachium, situated at the western termination of
that road, and opposite to Brundusium, a city on the Adriatic.
Philippi, also, was on the Egnatian road, 33 M.P. from Amphipolis, and 21 M.P. from Acontisma. As St. Paul twice visited
Philippi (Acts xvi. 12–40 and Acts xx. 6), it cannot be pre-

sumed that the Apostle himself was ignorant that this road, which he had in part seen and perhaps traversed, led to the Adriatic. St. Luke deliberately writing, after the Voyage had ended, was the companion of those who must have known that if they reached Illyrian Meleda, it was no great distance from Dyrrachium on the Adriatic Sea, and the difference between an island in the Adriatic Sea and an island in the African Sea cannot have been unknown to them.[1]

Not one single contemporary authority has been cited in contradiction of Pomponius Mela, Strabo, Lucan, Seneca, Pliny, Diodorus Siculus and Josephus.

Antecedent authority also confirms the nominal distinctions between the seas of Adria, Ionian and African.

SCYLAX, who is supposed to have lived B.C. 350, and who is mentioned by Aristotle, says, sec. 23 :—"Et insula maritimæ huic regioni propinqua est, cui nomen MELITA [*Meleda*]. Vicina huic est et alia insula, cui nomen 'Corcyra Nigra' [*Curzola*]. Et plurimum recedit [uno] promontorio hæc insula ab maritima regione : altero vero promontorio spectat versus Naronem [Narenta R.] fluvium. A MELITA abest [Corcyra] stadiis 20 : a maritima regione, stadiis 8."—Καὶ νῆσος τῆς παραλίας χώρας ἐγγύς, ᾗ ὄνομα, Μελίτη· καὶ ἑτέρα νῆσος ἐγγὺς ταύτης, ᾗ ὄνομα Κέρκυρα ἡ ' μέλαινα. Καὶ ἐρρέχει περὶ τὸ ἀκρωτήριον νῆσος αὕτη τῆς παραλίας χώρας σφόδρα, τῷ δὲ ἑτέρῳ ἀκρωτηρίῳ καθῆκει ἐπὶ τὸν Νάρωνα ποταμόν. Ἀπὸ δὲ τῆς Μελίτης ἀπέχει στάδια κ΄. τῆς δὲ παραλίας χώρας ἀπέχει στάδια η΄.—*Scylax*, sec. 23, ed. Gail. [The river Narenta falls into the Adriatic between the mainland and the long and narrow peninsula of Sabioncello. The island of Curzola is at the extremity of the sea end of this peninsula.] Under section 110 of Scylax, entitled "Car-

---

[1] Dr. Kitto stated (*Pictorial Bible*, 1838, iii. p. 319) "that it had been solidly shown by Beza, Bochart, Grotius, Wetstein, and others, from Ptolemy, *Strabo*, and others, that at the time in question, the *Adriatic Sea* was considered to comprehend the whole of the sea between Greece, Italy, *and Africa;* so that it (the Adriatic) comprised the Ionian, Cretan, and Sicilian seas!" The reader may estimate for himself the value of this statement. Dr. Kitto also refers to *Malta Illustrata*, folio, 1772, by Abela and Ciantar, lib. ii. n. 7, as containing sufficient illustrations from "ancient historians, geographers, and poets, showing the extent they assigned to the Adriatic Sea." If this Maltese work gave more information than is to be found elsewhere, Mr. Smith would have noticed it; but it gives no assistance.

thago," there is named "MELITA, *urbs cum portu.*" Melita Adri-
atica is therefore simply named "AN ISLAND," and Melita
Africana is mentioned by naming the "CITY OF MELITA AND
ITS PORT." He spoke of Meleda, as St. Luke speaks of it,
namely, as "an island" only, for it had no city and no port.
—*Scylax* : *Periplus* cura J. F. Gail, *Parisiis*, 1826, vol. i. p.
249. The expanse of sea, south of Adria, Scylax called the
Ionian Sea.

SCYMNUS of Chios, an early writer, but the time in which
he flourished is unknown, distinguished ADRIA from the IONIAN
SEA : "tanquam spectator non solum Græciæ, aut per Siciliam
sitarum urbium, sed testis ocularis factus etiam earum quæ
circa *Adriam* et earum quæ circa Ionium ordine sitæ sunt"
(ver. 129). According to the same writer : "SINUM ADRIATICUM
ferunt *barbarorum* multitudinem quandam circum habitare circulo
centum fere myriadibus quinquagintaque, regionem optimam
colentes et fructuosam : gemellos enim parere vel pecora aiunt.
Aër, qui transegit Ponticum mare, immutatur (flando) super
eos, quamvis [huic Ponto] proximos. Non enim nivosus, neque
valde frigidus, humidus vero omnino assidue manet, subitus,
turbulentusque invadens ad mutationes, *præsertim æstate igneo-*
rumque turbinum et jactus fulminum, dictosque illic TYPHONES."
—*Scymni Orbis Descriptio*, ver. 374 ; trans. Lat. Gail.

JUSTINUS also, who is supposed to have flourished at the
end of the fourth century, so far as he represents Trogus Pom-
peius who was alive B.C. 20, may be cited, He says, "*Adria*
quoque Illyrico mari proxima, quæ et ADRIATICO MARI nomen
dedit, Græca urbs est."—*Justinus*, lib. xx. sec. 1.

CICERO, in writing to Atticus (lib. ix. Epist. 19, B.C. 58),
says, "The Adriatic Sea being *closely guarded*, I shall sail
by the Tyrrhenian, and if the passage from Puteoli be difficult, I shall make my way to Croton or Thurii."

The purpose of citing authorities anterior in date to the
time of the Voyage, is to show the distinctness of the separation of the Adriatic, by this name, from the name of the southern
sea, and to affirm that up to the very time of the Voyage, the
name "Adria" was not extended to include the southern sea.

We now come to writers who were not contemporaries with
St. Paul, but on whose statements depend the affirmations of

those who say the expanse of sea south of the Adriatic Gulf was at the time of the Voyage called " Adria."—T. F.]

PTOLEMY.

[Ptolemy was alive A.D. 161, and, therefore, is not to be cited as having the authority of a contemporary writer; yet those who affirm that Malta was the scene of the shipwreck, cite him as their chief witness, and they do so very unfairly. They omit, also, to say that APPIAN and AULUS GELLIUS were alive A.D. 161, for from their writings they can get no aid.

In order to place beyond dispute the boundary of the Adriatic Sea, as given by Ptolemy, it is as well to cite that writer step by step. The word Πέλαγος is used throughout, and Liddell and Scott (3rd edit. p. 1083) say: " Πέλαγος strictly is to θάλασσα as a part to the whole, and, therefore, often takes an epithet from the adjoining countries." [m] Ptolemy uses the word πέλαγος in the following instances, when " sea " is named, as respects the Adriatic :—[n]

1. Lib. ii. ch. 15, p. 164, speaking of the boundary of Illyria, he names τὸν 'Αδρίαν κόλπον, τὸν 'Αδρίαν and τοῦ 'Αδρίου πλευρὰ. Among the Dalmatian islands he names " MELITE " (page 168), now called " MELEDA."

2. Bk. iii. ch. 1, p. 171, he uses the words τοῦ 'Αδρίου κόλπου; Magna Græcia he places on the Adriatic Sea ['Αδριατικὸν πέλαγος] (p. 174); Calabria on the Ionian Sea ['Ιώνιον πέλαγος] (p. 174) ; Apulia on the Ionian Sea [ἐν 'Ιωνίῳ πελάγει] (p. 175), including Garganus ; then northward he names places on the Adriatic Gulf [κόλπον] ; then coasting round the north

---

[m] In that essay of falsehood, the apocryphal *Acts of the Holy Apostles Peter and Paul*, it is said, " that after Paul went out of the island Gaudomeleta, he came to Italy."—Translation by Alexander Walker, ed. 1870. The writer of the " Acts " describes Simon, the magician, flying in the air!

[n] The word πέλαγος is used by Ptolemy in describing a border sea—not the whole sea. It is also used by St. Luke in speaking of the border sea of Cilicia and Pamphylia. The word θάλασσα is used in the New Testament when the sea generally, or the whole sea, is spoken of—as " cast into the sea," the " Red Sea," the " sea of Galilee and Tiberias," "boat in the sea," " wheat into the sea," " sand of the sea," " escaped the sea." The Adriatic is described by Ptolemy as a border sea [πέλαγος].

he places Istria and Pola in this gulf; he describes the line of
the Apennines towards "Adria" [τῷ 'Αδρίᾳ] to Mons Garganus.
The Diomedian Islands, off the coast of Apulia, he places in the
Ionian Sea (p. 187).

3. Bk. iii. ch. 3, p. 190, the southern boundary of SARDINIA
is stated to be the *African* Sea [τοῦ 'Αφρικανοῦ]. "Sardinia insula cingitur ab oriente Tyrrheno mari [τοῦ Τυῤῥηνικοῦ πελά-
γους], a meridie mari Africano, ab occidente vero Sardoo mari,
a septentrionibus denique eo mari, quod inter ipsam et Cyrnum
insulam interiacet."

4. Bk. iii. ch. 4, p. 193, SICILY is described to be bounded
on the south by the AFRICAN Sea [τοῦ 'Αφρικανοῦ], and on the
east by the Adriatic Sea [τοῦ 'Αδρίου πελάγους].

5. Bk. iii. ch. 12, p. 218, Macedonia is described to be
bounded on the west by the *Ionian* Sea [τῷ 'Ιωνίῳ πελάγει] from
Dyrrachium or Epidamnus to the river Celydnus on the
northern boundary of Epirus.

6. Bk. iii. ch. 13 [14], pp. 226, 227, Epirus is described to
be bounded on the west by the *Ionian* Sea [τοῦ 'Ιωνίου πελά-
γους], "occidentale latus finitur Ionii quæ est ad Acrocerau-
nios montes;" then, mentioning Oricum, Panormus, Onchesmus
and Cassiope in Chaonia, it is said, "meridianum latus finitur
Adriatico mari ['Αδριατικῷ πελάγει] ab eo termino ad Ache-
loum usque fluvium," and included among the islands of Epirus,
Corcyra, Cephallenia, and Zacynthus.

7. Bk. iii. ch. 14, p. 229, Achaia is bounded on the south
by the Adriatic Sea.

8. Bk. iii. ch. 14 [15,16], p. 236, the Peloponnesus is bounded
on the west and south by the Adriatic Sea [τῷ 'Αδριατικῷ πελάγει],
and on the east by the Cretan Sea [τῷ Κρητικῷ πελάγει].

That Ptolemy should have placed the Ionian Sea within the
limits of the Adriatic (bk. iii. ch. 1), and have placed the
Adriatic south of the Ionian Sea, namely, south of Macedonia
(ch. 12) and of Epirus (ch. 13), may fairly lead it to be inferred that he is no reliable authority on the limits of the
Adriatic. At all events he is opposed to all contemporary
authority existing at the time of the Voyage, and to his own
contemporaries, Appian and Aulus Gellius; but those who rely
on him hide from their readers what he says of Malta being in
the African Sea.

9. Bk. iii. ch. 15 [16, 17], p. 242, the island of Crete is said to be bounded on the west by the Adriatic Sea [τοῦ 'Λδρια- τικοῦ πελάγους], on the north by the Cretan Sea, on the south by the Libyan Sea, and on the east by the Carpathian Sea [τοῦ Καρπαθίου πελάγους].

The only island named MELITE in these parts of the Medi- terranean Sea, named by Ptolemy the ADRIATIC, is the island MELITE on the Dalmatian coast (lib. ii. ch. 15, p. 168).

When APPIAN (who lived about the year A.D. 138, and at the same time as Ptolemy) named the whole sea, he said, "Passing to the other side, the Romans govern other nations about the Pontus,—namely the European Mysi, and the Thracians on the borders of the Euxine. From Ionia (westward) is a gulf of the sea [θαλάσσης],—namely, the Ægean; then another gulf of the sea [θαλάσσης] the Ionian and the Sicilian passage [πορθμός]; and the Tyrrhene Sea as far as the Pillars of Her- cules." (Pref. 3.) His omission to name the Adriatic shows the common name used to describe the expanse of the sea to have been the Ionian. In his preface to the Illyrian War he describes the Liburnians to have been good seamen, and to have plundered the islands and ships on the Ionian Sea [De Bell. Illyricis, ch. 3; Bekker. Teubner, ed. 1852, vol. i. p. 424] —καὶ ναυτικοὶ μὲν ἐπὶ τοῖς 'Αρδιαίκοις ἐγένοντο Λιβυρνοὶ γένος ἕτερον' Ἰλλυριῶν, οἳ τὸν 'Ιόνιον καὶ τὰς νήσους ἐλῃστεύον ναυσὶν ὠκείαις τε καὶ κούραις]. Being contemporary with Ptolemy, and being born at Alexandria where also Ptolemy was supposed to be born and certainly resided, and afterwards having lived at Rome [καὶ δίκαις ἐν 'Ρώμῃ συναγορεύσας ἐπὶ τῶν βασιλέων, Hist. Præf.], his authority is at least equal to that of Ptolemy. He certainly did not call the sea between Sicily and Crete, the Adriatic, but he did call it the Ionian.

AULUS GELLIUS, who lived under Hadrian, Antoninus Pius, and Marcus Aurelius (A.D. 117–180) in the passage cited at page 18, ante, also calls the sea from the west of Epirus, south of Corcyra to Brundusium, the Ionian, and he also may have lived 'at the same period of time as Ptolemy.

Ptolemy (bk. iv. ch. 3, p. 260) describes a northern por- tion of Africa (τῆς 'Αφρικῆς) from the river Ampsaga (Suf- jima) to the Greater Syrtis, to be bounded by the AFRICAN Sea; and at the end of the chapter, the following AFRICAN islands are said to be in the sea; or in the Latin translation of Wilberg (p. 272):—

"In alto insulæ sunt Africæ (Πελάγιαι δὲ νῆσοί εἰσι τῆς Ἀφρικῆς αἵδε) hæ:
Cossyra, insula et oppidum (πόλις) (*Pantellaria*);
Glauconis insula et oppidum:
Melite (*Malta*) insula, in qua est (Μελίτη νῆσος, ἐν ᾗ)
Melite oppidum (πόλις),
et peninsula (χερσόνησος):
et Junonis fanum (ἱερόν),
et Herculis fanum" (ἱερόν).

So not merely is Malta described to be an AFRICAN island, but Ptolemy most distinctly places it in the AFRICAN Sea, having also, as before mentioned (lib. iii. ch. 4), said that Sicily was bounded on the south by the AFRICAN Sea.[o]

As Ptolemy represented Sicily and Sardinia to be bounded on the south by the African Sea, it is impossible to comprehend the conclusion that Ptolemy is an authority for saying, that at the end of fourteen days' sailing, to the west of the Peloponnesus, the ship was in the Adriatic Sea at Malta! Yet this is the inference, notwithstanding its manifest absurdity, of those who refer to Ptolemy, in order to sustain their peculiar argument in favour of Malta.

Strabo also, in describing the coast of AFRICA (bk. xvii. ch. 3, sec. 16), after speaking of Carthage, says, "MELITE (*Malta*), an island, is 500 stadia distant from Cossuros. Then follows the city of Adrumes (Sousah) with a naval arsenal; then the Taracheiæ, numerous small islands; then the city Thrapsus (Demass), and near it Lopadussa (Lampedusa), an island situated far from the coast; then the promontory of

---

[o] See also plates 84 and 85 of Victor Langlois' edition of the photographic copy of the MSS. of Ptolemy in the monastery of Vatopedi, Mount Athos, made by Sewastionoff, 1867; and *Ptolemy*, lib. viii. tab. 2. Mr. Smith said (p. 160) that Mr. Bryant "adduced the authority of Ptolemy often enough when it answered his purpose, and passes over those parts of the work which bear directly on the question in total silence." This statement may be condemned in the strongest language as erroneous. What are we to say to Mr. Smith's suppression of what Ptolemy relates of Malta being an African island in the African sea?

Ammon Balithon, near which is a look-out for the approach
of the thunny, then the city of Thena (Thaini), lying at the
entrance of Little Syrtis." (Falconer's translation, vol. iii.
p. 288.) Ptolemy and Strabo most certainly and clearly are
no authorities from which to infer, that if at the end of fourteen
days the ship was at Malta, it was also in the Adriatic!—T. F.]

PAUSANIAS.

[Nothing can more strongly exhibit the desperate difficulty
in which those writers are placed, who wish to represent the
expanse of the Mediterranean Sea between Sicily and Greece
to have been called the "Adriatic" or "Adria," than their citation of Pausanias. He was alive A.D. 170, and, therefore, he
also cannot be cited as a contemporary authority. He mentions (lib. v. ch. 25, p. 1; Schubart, p. 412; Teubner, 1853)
that "a great misfortune once befell the Messenians who inhabit the coast. They had sent to a festival at Rhegium,
according to an annual and ancient custom, a chorus of thirty-
five youths, with a chorus leader and piper. The ship in which
they had embarked sank with the passengers, and was seen
no more. For the sea (θάλασσα) in the passage [between
Messene and Rhegium] is of all the most stormy ; it is agitated
by the winds which come from both sides [of Italy] and bring
the waves OUT of Adria and OUT of the other sea (πέλαγος) called
the Tyrrhene Sea." In this passage the word "Adria" is clearly
limited to the Adriatic. [Ἔστι γὰρ δὴ ἡ κατὰ τοῦτον θάλασσα
τὸν πορθμὸν θαλάσσης χειμεριωτάτη πάσης. οἵ τε γὰρ ἄνεμοι
ταράσσουσιν αὐτήν, ἀμφοτέρωθεν τὸ κῦμα ἐπάγοντες ΕΚ τοῦ
Ἀδρίου καὶ ΕΚ ἑτέρου πελάγους ὃ καλεῖται Τυρσηνόν.]
The legend of the river Alpheus is also told by Pausanias
(Arcad. lib. viii. ch. 54):—"The Alpheus, in comparison
with other rivers, shows a peculiar character, for it frequently
disappears under ground, and then rises up again. Advancing
from Phylace [*Krya Vrysi*] and the place called Symbola
[the junction], it [the *Saranda*] descends into the plain of
Tegea; then rising in Ascræa, and uniting its stream with
Eurotas, it descends a second time into the earth [*passing under
a mountain called Tzimbanu*]. Then rising in a place [*Mar-*

mara ?] where the Arcadians gave it the name of Pegæ (or the fountains), and passing along the territory of Pisæ and Olympia, it discharges itself into the sea above Cyllene, a naval arsenal of Elis. Nor does Adria afterwards *prevent its advancing onwards,* for it makes a passage even through this sea (πέλαγος), great and violent as it is; and in the island of Ortygia, in front of Syracuse, shows itself still the Alpheus, and unites its waters with the fountain of Arethusa." [p] There is nothing in this passsage to show that the name of Adria extended to the sea south of Sicily; or that the sea between CRETE AND MALTA was known by that name; and in the previous passage [ch. 25] Pausanias says, "the winds bring the waves *out* of Adria and *out* of the Tyrrhene :"—not that the southern sea [θάλασσα] was "Adria." It was πέλαγος not θάλασσα, which he designated to be "Adria" in his reference to this sea. As the waves were driven out of Adria and out of the Tyrrhene seas, they were not driven *into* such seas: therefore, such seas were not to the south. So the words, "preventing its advancing on-

---

[p] [The following explains the latter part of what is cited from Pausanias:—
"When standing on the shore near the fountain of Arethusa, I observed, in the middle of the port of Syracuse, that rounded surface such as is occasioned by water rushing up from beneath. I was told it was a fresh-water spring, in the sea. As this and the Arethusa are near one another, the waters might mix, and the fresh water springing up from the bottom of the sea might easily be said by the Greeks to be the river Alpheus itself." (MSS.)

Again (MSS.): "At a little distance from the fountain of Arethusa is a very large spring of fresh water in the sea. It is called *Occhi di Zilica.*"—"As this spring is not taken notice of by any of the great number of ancients who speak of Arethusa, it is most probable it is part of that fountain which has, since they wrote, burst out before its arrival at the island of Ortygia."—*Brydone's Travels.* Syracuse, June 1.

" Quis Catinam sileat ? Quis quadruplices Syracusas ?
Hanc ambustorum fratrum pietate celebrem,
Illam complexam miracula fontis et amnis.
Quam MARIS IONII subter vada salsa meantes
Consociant dulces placita sibi sede liquores,
Incorruptarum miscentes oscula aquarum."

Ausonii Claræ Urbes, xi.

Ausonius, who thus calls the expanse of sea the Ionian, was alive A.D. 388, is one of those late writers after the Voyage who could not, with propriety, be cited if he had been opposed to writers of the first century of the Christian era respecting the name of the sea between Sicily and Greece, or the name by which it was known A.D. 60.—T. F.]

wards" show that the waves on the eastern side only of the Mediterranean are referred to; a special course of resistance separate for the expanse of the sea (p. 53).

Pausanias is cited at length, though what he says simply shows that the sea, called by him and by Ptolemy the Adriatic, was not that between Sicily and the coast of Africa, or including Malta.

In the 'Life of St. Paul' (vol. ii. p. 427, by the Very Rev. the Dean of Chester), it is mentioned that Pausanias says, "the Straits of Messina *unite* the Tyrrhene Sea with the Adriatic Sea." There is no doubt of this fact if "unite" means that a ship can sail from the one sea to the other, but it proves nothing. The author of that work could have found a much better illustration than the one he has chosen. Whoever wrote the martyrdom of St. Ignatius, Bishop of the Church of Antioch, (and, according to Chrysostom, a Bishop by the choice of the Apostles,) the genuineness of which is recognised (see Smith's *Biogr. Dict.* vol. ii. p. 564), gives this account of his route to Rome; namely, that he went from Antioch to Seleucia, thence to Smyrna, where he visited Polycarp; from Smyrna to Troas; then going to Neapolis, he went on foot by Philippi, through Macedonia, and on to that part of Epirus which is near Epidamnus [Dyrrachium—Durazzo—41° 18′ N. lat. and 19° 26′ E. long.], and finding a ship in one of the ports, he *sailed over the Adriatic Sea* and *entering from it on the Tyrrhene*, he passed by various islands and cities, naming Puteoli only, and sailed to the Roman harbour." He sailed from the Adriatic to the Tyrrhene Sea, but this does not mean, that all the sea between either was called "Tyrrhene" or "Adriatic," or that either of these named seas extended to the south of the island of Sicily.

"Tyrrhenos igitur fluctus, lateque sonantem
Pertulit Ionium."—*Juvenal*, Sat. vi. *v.* 92.

"Sonat in Ionio vagus Adria ponto."—
Lucanus, lib. v. 613.

In which part of the Ionian Sea were the waves of the Tyrrhene or of Adria to be found at the end of fourteen days' sail from Crete? [καὶ ἀπὸ τοῦ Ἰονίου παρήκουσα ἐπὶ πλεῖστον τῆς Τυρρηνικῆς θαλάσσης, *Appiani Hist. Præf.* about A.D. 140.]

St. Ignatius died A.D. 107 or 116, or upwards of forty years before Ptolemy. [*The Writings of the Apostolic Fathers,* Edinburgh, 1867, p. 295; [q] translated by the Rev. Dr. Roberts, Dr. Donaldson, and the Rev. F. Crombie.] It will not be contested that Malta was south of the Tyrrhene Sea, and not in the Tyrrhene.

Mr. Smith says " that Procopius placed Melite on the verge of the Adriatic Sea." Then Procopius did not place Malta in the Adriatic Sea, and Procopius could not have been accepted as an authority if he had written otherwise, for he was not born until the beginning of the *sixth* century; he flourished about A.D. 527. Why cite Procopius, if writers earlier than Ptolemy or Pausanias had made the fact clear? Why not have named such writers, if they could have been named? Then, again, Mr. Smith stated (p. 159, *n.*) that " commentators [*i. e.* Dr. Falconer] gravely tell us that, because Ptolemy calls ' Melite ' an African island, it cannot be in the Adriatic Sea." The gravity of truth does not throw a doubt on the fact, for Ptolemy distinctly placed the island in the African Sea ; and, as he placed it in the African Sea, he did not place it in the Adriatic Sea.

But more than this : the above paragraph in this Dissertation commences with a reference to Ptolemy. He was cited to show that he called Malta an *African* island, and it might have appeared to most men that it was needless to add that Ptolemy further stated,—it was in the *African* Sea. Mr. Smith (p. 167) says, " L Avocat does not, as Bryant and Falconer have done, pass over the *unequivocal* testimony of Ptolemy in silence." But Dr. Falconer was not silent. He cited Ptolemy to show that he described Malta to be an *African* island; and he might have further said the great geographer in the most distinct words placed it in the African Sea. There was no occasion to say more than that Ptolemy described it to be an African island, and this it was, according to Ptolemy, both as regarded territory and as regarded the sea which surrounded it. Ptolemy distinctly and " unequivocally " excluded the island

---

[q] *The Writings of the Apostolic Fathers,* (Edinburgh, ed. 1867, p. 295) Ante-Nicene Christian Library, by the Rev. Dr. Roberts, Dr. Donaldson, and the Rev. F. Crombie.

from all seas but that of Africa, in which, indeed, he expressly and by name included it. In such a state of facts Mr. Smith imputed absence of good faith—"silence"—*i.e.* suppression of something—to one of the most truthful, candid, and unevasive of men. And what are we to say respecting the use by Mr. Smith of the words "unequivocal testimony" when the testimony of Ptolemy is so distinctly opposed to what is represented to be its effect?

It is not to be imputed to St. Luke, whose words are most expressive and accurate, that he was ignorant that Malta was, in his time, known to be part of Africa and in the "African Sea." He gives the names of the border seas of Cilicia and Pamphylia. Why, therefore, without any assignable reason, should we impute to him a disregard or want of knowledge of the African Sea, and say he called it the Adriatic? It is also a strong reason why St. Luke should not have been misled in his use of the word "Adria" with reference to the African Sea, that there was with him Aristarchus, a Macedonian of Thessalonica: and St. Paul had been to Thessalonica (Acts xviii. 1). The Macedonian, and even St. Paul, cannot be presumed to have been ignorant that Dyrrachium, the chief western port of Macedonia, being the termination of the Via Egnatia from Thessalonica (Strabo, lib. viii.; trans. vol. i. p. 495) was south of Melite in the Adriatic; nor is it probable he would have said an African island was to be found in the sea called "Adria." "When it was day *they* knew not the land" (xxvii. 39). That Alexandrian sailors should have failed to recognise Malta, if they had reached that island, has always caused remark, and Major Reynell acknowledged the difficulty it suggested (Smith, p. 145). "When they or we were escaped" (ch. viii. ver. 1) the Vatican MS. reads:—"then *we* [not, as in our version, *they*] knew the island was called Melite." The sailors might not have known that even an island "was nearing them,"—what "country" it was; "but *then*"—the island being, no doubt, named,—"WE knew it was called Melite." The Spanish version has "supimos"—"we knew."—T. F.]

CAPELLA.

[Martianus Capella flourished before the year A.D. 439. These are passages from his work :—

"Nam solutis Alpium niuibus flagrantia solis æstiui exuberat ultra gurgitis ripas nullique gloriæ nobilium amnium cedens triginta receptis fluminibus *Adriaticum* mare magna opimus granditate perfundit."—Lib. vi. p. 215 (Eyssenhardt), Teubner ed. 1866.

" Egressos sinu Ambracio in Ionium."—Lib. vi. p. 221, line 6.

"Peloponnesum pæne insula inter duo maria Ægeum et Ionium."—Lib. vi. p. 221, line 17.

He therefore did not represent the sea south of the Adriatic to be otherwise than the Ionian. The sea immediately on the southern shore of Italy he calls the Ausonian :—

" Hic primus Europæ sinus Ausonii maris patet nonaginta sex milibus, quique tres sinus habet. Italiæ frons incipit, quæ Magna Græcia appellata est, ubi amnium et oppidorum copia." —Lib. vi. p. 219.—T. F.]

ARATOR.

[The earliest known Latin writer who connected the name of St. Paul with the island of Malta is Arator, who is said to have been born about the year A.D. 490, and to have been alive in the sixth century, namely A.D. 554. He, therefore, could have had no more information on the geography of the Mediterranean than we possess.

> " His dictis ruit ira maris, sublataque dudum
> Lux revocata micat, velamine noctis aperto
> Pandere visa solum, quod præbuit hospita nautis
> *Sicanio* latere renuis vicina *Melite*. . . .
> Mensibus hibernis tribus in regione *Miletum*
> Multiplicem dat *Paulus* opem, Publique parentem
> Finitima de clade levat, quo munere viso
> Undique præcipites subitam rapuere salutem." '

—T. F.]

' *Aratoris Subdiaconi, Romanæ Ecclesiæ Cardinalis in Apostolorum Acta; Collectio Pisaurensis.* Pisauri, 1766. 4to. Vol. vi. p. 155.

CONSTANTINUS VII.

[The earliest known writer who connected the name of St. Paul with the island of Meleda was Constantinus VII., Emperor of the East A.D. 911–959, usually known as "Constantinus Porphyrogenitus," and who was born A.D. 905. In his work *De Administrando Imperio*, ch. 34–36, he says, "The country which the Pagani now inhabit was formerly under the power of those Romans whom Diocletian (born A.D. 245) transferred from Rome and settled in Dalmatia. The Pagani descend from the unbaptized Servi, and from under that prince who fled to Heraclius for protection. The country was seized upon and laid waste by the 'Arabi,' but it was again settled with inhabitants under Heraclius. They are called 'Pagani' because they did not accept baptism at the time when all the Servi were baptized, for the word, Pagani means, in the Servian dialect, 'unbaptized.' In the Roman dialect the country is called Arenta, and hence the people are called Arentani by the Romans. In Pagani are inhabited towns, namely Mocrum, Berulla, Ostroc, and Labinetza. The Arentani hold possession of the following islands : The great island Curcra, or Corcyra [Nigra?], in which is a town. *Also another large island, Meleta, or Malozeatæ, which is mentioned by St. Luke in the Acts of the Apostles, who calls it Melite. It was here a viper fixed itself on the finger of St. Paul, who burnt it in the fire."*—T. F.]

To the present day, the tradition on the shores of the Adriatic in favour of Meleda is as strong as that which prevails at Malta in favour of that island.

[Admiral Smyth, in his work on ' The Mediterranean ' (p. 34) has commented on the question thus :—" Thucydides tells us (lib. i.) that Epidamnus, now Durazzo, is a city on the right-hand as you sail into the Ionian Gulf : it is the *Hadriacas undas* of Virgil ; while Horace makes the *Arbiter* Adriæ wash the Calabrian coast ; and Pliny, who calls the Adriatic the second gulf of Europe, expressly places Lavinia and the town of Croton, both of Calabria Ultra, on its shores. Strabo describes the Iapygian and Ceraunian shores at the line of separation in these divisions. He admits that the mouth or strait belongs to both, yet it is obvious that the lower part was colonised from Ionia, the upper from Adria. The name, therefore, of the first part of this sea is termed Ionian, and the inner part, up to its recesses, '*Adriatic*;' but 'now,' he says,—[*circa* A.D. 18] 'the latter is the name even of the whole sea.' [The word is '*κόλ-πον*,' not *θάλασσα* nor *πέλαγος*!—T. F.] This statement," Admiral Smyth continues, "is strengthened by the fact of the Gulf of Venice being called the Upper Sea (Mare Superum) by the Latin writers. In a splendid copy of Ptolemy lent to me by his late Royal Highness the Duke of Sussex, which was printed at Rome in the year 1478, 'Mare Adriaticum' appears in uncial characters on *tabula secunda* in the space between Sicilia and Corcyra; on *tabula sexta* it is below Bruttium and Messene; on *tabula septima* it is marked in the offing of Leontium in Sicily, and on the tenth plate it is opposite to the space between Zacynthos and the Strophades."[t]

No person could have been better informed than Admiral Smyth of the unreliable character of any ancient map; but the value of any engraved map of the year 1478 is extinguished by the plates 84 and 85 of Victor Langlois' edition of Ptolemy, which is a photographic copy of an ancient MS. of Ptolemy, found in the monastery of Vatopedi, Mount Athos, made by Sewastionoff in 1867, and which agrees with Table ii. lib. viii., engraved in the edition of Bucher.[u]

---

* If St. Paul knew there was one certain island on which they would be wrecked, he or the sailors would, in all probability, have known it by name, had it been Malta, before they landed. If one of several islands were in sight in part of a sea, namely, in Adria, not previously known to the sailors, it would have been improbable they could have nominated the island on which they were wrecked until by some means it had been distinguished from other islands.—T. F.]

[t] " Κόλπος, a bay or gulf of the sea; κόλφος, *Mod. Gr.*; Golfo, *Ital.*; Gulf, *Engl.*; and it corresponds in all senses with the Latin word *Sinus*."—*Liddell and Scott's Dict.* 6th ed. p. 865.

[u] We do not know what were the original maps of Ptolemy, but we may assume they did not contradict his own writings. The following is from the article " Agathodaemon " (*Smith's Dict. of Greek and Roman Biography*, vol. i. p. 65):—" 'AGATHODAEMON,' a native of Alexandria. All that is known of him is that he was a designer of some maps to accompany Ptolemy's Geography. Copies of these maps are found appended to several MSS. of Ptolemy. One of these is at Vienna and another at Venice. At the end of each of these MSS. is a notice in Greek, that ' Agathodaemon of Alexandria delineated the

"Hence," says Admiral Smyth, continuing his argument, "it is evident that the Adriatic Sea was held to be that vast expanse of water contained in the Upper, the Ionian, and the Sicilian Seas; in fact, that it extended both to the north and south, from the narrows which some have chosen to assume as its mouth. But these were convertible terms; *for* as we have just seen, Thucydides cites the position of Epidamnus [Dyrrachium] as in the Ionian waters, and St. Paul's ship was driven 'up and down in Hadria.' [A mistranslation of διαφερομένων ἡμῶν ἐν τῷ Ἀδρίᾳ.—T. F.] 'The Adriatic Sea,' says Hesychius, ' is the same with the Ionian Sea,' a definition that might have suppressed arguments, which have been conducted with more vehemence than judgment."

There are no premises to justify the word "hence;" the mistranslation destroys the second statement, and as Hesychius was not alive until some four hundred years after the voyage, his opinion is of no value, being contradicted by the writers contemporary with the Voyage already cited.

Strabo called the whole sea between Sicily and Crete the *Sicilian* Sea. The words cited by Admiral Smyth he evidently did not understand, and he seems to have been unaware of the following passages of the same author :—

"The Sea of Sicily washes Italy from the Straits of Rhegium to Locris, and also the Eastern coast of Sicily from Messene to Syracuse and Pachynus. On the eastern side it reaches to the promontories of Crete, surrounds the greater part of the Peloponnesus, and fills the Gulf of Corinth. On the north, it advances to the Iapygian Promontory, the mouth of the *Ionian*

whole of the inhabited world, according to the eight books of Geography of Claudius Ptolemy.' The Vienna MS. of Ptolemy is one of the most beautiful extant. Heeren, however, considers the delineator of the maps to have been a contemporary of Ptolemy, who (viii. l. 2) mentions certain maps or tables (πίνακες) which agree in number and arrangement with those of Agathodaemon in the MSS. Various errors crept into copies of the maps of Agathodaemon, and Nicholaus Donis, a Benedictine monk, who flourished about A.D. 1470, corrected them, substituting Latin for Greek names. His maps are appended to the Ebnerian MS. of Ptolemy. They are the same in number, and really the same in order, with those of Agathodaemon." (Heeren, *Commentatio de Fontibus Geograph. Ptolemaei Tabularum iis annexarum*; Raidel, *Commentatio critico-literaria de Claud. Ptolemaei Geographia de Cl. Ptolemaei Geographia ejusque codicibus*, p. 7.) This article was written by Mr. C. P. Mason.

Gulf, the southern parts of Epirus, as far as the Ambracic Gulf, and the continuation of the coast which forms the Corinthian Gulf, near the Peloponnesus."—*Strabo*, bk. ii. ch. 5, sec. 20 ; translation, vol. i. p. 186.

"The Adriatic stretches north and west; it is long and narrow, being in length about 6000 stadia, and its greatest breadth 1200.

" The Sea of Sicily is said to be about 4500 stadia from Pachynus (Cape Passaro, south-east of Sicily) to Crete, and the same distance to Tænarus (Cape Matapan) in Laconia (a southern point of the Peloponnesus).

"Next to the Sea of Sicily are the Cretan, Saronic (Gulf of Egina, part of the Ægæan Sea) and Myrtoan (south of Attica and Eubœa) Seas comprised between Crete, Argeia (in the Peloponnesus) and Attica (part of modern Livadia). Adjacent to these are the Ægæan Sea, the Gulf of Melas, the Hellespont, the Icarian and Carpathian Seas " (*Strabo*, translation, bk. ii. ch. 5, sec. 20, 21). "From Sunium [Cape Kolónnes on the southern coast of Attica] to the Peloponnesus are the Myrtoan, the Cretan, and the Libyan Seas, together with the gulfs as as far as the SICILIAN Sea, which comprise the gulfs of Ambracia, of Corinth, and of Crissa" [the inner sea of the Corinthian Gulf].—*Strabo*, bk. vii. ch. 7, sec. 6 ; translation, vol. i. p. 496.

Writing of Crete, (bk. xviii. ch. 4, sec. 2) Strabo says, "it is washed on the north by the Ægæan and Cretan seas, and on the south by the African, which joins the Egyptian Sea."

"Continuous to the Icarian Sea, towards the south is the Carpathian Sea and the Egyptian Sea [adjoins] to this: to the west are the Cretan and African seas." (Bk. x. ch. 5, sec. 13.)

The Sicilian and Cretan Seas were, therefore, according to Strabo, south of the Adriatic, and as respects the African Sea, Ptolemy and Strabo agree, and they both place Malta in the African Sea.

It is, therefore, clear that Admiral Smyth had no authority which can be accepted to justify his conclusions ; on the other side, Mr. Bryant remarks that "The Adriatic Sea, in early ages, comprehended only the upper part of the ' *Sinus Ionius*,' where were a city and a river [now, in 1872, fifteen miles inland], both called 'ADRIA,' from one of which it took its name. It afterwards was advanced deeper in the gulf, but never so engrossed it as to obliterate its name; for it was called 'Sinus' and 'Mare Adriaticum,' and 'SINUS' and 'MARE IONIUM' by writers for many ages." Herodotus (born B.C. 484) calls the whole the "Ionian Gulf," without limitation. Ἐκ δὲ τοῦ κόλπου τοῦ Ἰονίου Ἀμφίμνηστος Ἐπιστρόφου Ἐπιδάμνιος· οὗτος δὲ ἐκ τοῦ Ἰονίου κόλπου (lib. vi. ch. 127)—"From the Ionian Gulf Amphimnestus, son of Epistrophus, an Epidamnian; he came from the Ionian Gulf."

Thucydides (born B.C. 471) speaks of it in the same manner: Ἐπίδαμνός ἐστι πόλις ἐν δεξιᾷ ἐσπλέοντι τὸν Ἰόνιον κόλπον (lib. i. ch. 24). "Epidamnus (Durazzo) is a city on the right-hand on sailing into the Ionian Gulf." It was esteemed the same in the days of Theophrastus (B.C. 322, Hist. Plan. lib. viii. ch. 10). Ἐν Ἀπολλωνίᾳ γοῦν τῇ περὶ τὸν Ἰόνιον οὐκ ἐσθίεσθαί φασιν ὅλως κύαμον.

But when the Romans came to navigate this "Sinus" they were more acquainted with the "Adria," and called it according to that name, allotting to the Ionian only the lower part of the gulf. And Greek writers who lived under the Roman influence copied them therein. Hence Polybius (who flourished B.C. 167) speaking of Italy (lib. ii. Res Gallicæ, ed. Teubner, vol. i. p. 134), says, Τῆς δὴ συμπάσης Ἰταλίας τῷ σχήματι τριγωνοειδοῦς ὑπαρχούσης, τὴν μὲν μίαν ὀρίζει πλευρὰν αὐτῆς τὴν πρὸς ἀνατολὰς κεκλιμένην ὅ τ' Ἰόνιος πόρος [passage] καὶ κατὰ τὸ συνεχὲς ὁ κατὰ τὸν Ἀδρίαν κόλπος, τὴν δὲ πρὸς μεσημβρίαν καὶ δυσμὰς τετραμμένην τὸ Σικελικὸν καὶ Τυρρηνικὸν πέλαγος—"to the east Italy is bounded by the Ionian strait or passage [πόρος], and the gulf [κόλπος] of Adria, which is contiguous to and above it, and south and west by the Sicilian and Tyrrhenian Sea [πέλαγος not θάλασσα]. He then proceeds to inform us, that the Ionian Strait reached south to the promontory of Cocynthus in Bruttia, where was the commencement of the Sicilian " Sea : τὸ προκείμενον ἀκρωτήριον τῆς Ἰταλίας εἰς

---

* Hampton (vol. i. p. 117, 5th ed. 1823) has translated Ἰόνιος πόρος, "the Ionian sea," but πόρος has not this meaning. (Lib. v. ch. 110.) The word means, a narrow part of the sea, a strait, a passage-way, as was the Ἰόνιος πόρος from Greece to Italy. (Liddell and Scott's Dict. p. 1314.)

τὴν μεσημβρίαν, ὃ προσαγορεύεται μὲν Κόκυνθος διαρεῖ δὲ τὸν Ἰόνιον πόρον [passage] καὶ τὸ Σικελικὸν πέλαγος (lib. ii. ch. 14; Teubner, vol. i. p. 135). As it extended northward it comprehended the island Saso, which was situated in its entrance upwards: νῆσον ἣ καλεῖται μὲν Σάσων· κεῖται δὲ κατὰ τὴν εἰσβολὴν τὴν εἰς τὸν Ἰόνιον πόρον [passage]. (Lib. v. ch. 110; Teubner, ed. Dindorfii, vol. ii. p. 229.)

Thus we have three seas, the "*Adriatic*," the "*Ionian*," and "*Sicilian*," very clearly specified. As yet we are a great way from Malta. Besides the Ionian Gulf, which I should choose to distinguish by the title of the "*Upper Ionian*," there was another sea of that name, below, which occupied the whole space between Sicily and Greece, as well as between Bruttia and Epirus. This was the "*Ionium Magnum*," or the "*Ionian Sea*." It began at Tænarus and reached the Ceraunian mountains. This must be carefully distinguished from that above. It was called by some, the "*Sicilian Sea*," and by others, the "*Cretan*," but properly comprehended both.—*Bryant*, bk. xvii.

The precision of these remarks, and the support they receive from Polybius, is a strong contrast with the statement of Admiral Smyth above cited; though no intelligent person can feel otherwise than respectful towards the memory of Admiral Smyth, or can be disposed to disparage the value of his eminent public services in the Mediterranean Sea.—T. F.]

HORACE.

[The late Very Rev. Dean Alford having, in his revised version of the New Testament (1870, p. 208), printed the following note to verse 27 of the Acts, ch. xxvii., referring to the word "Adria:"—

"*Not what is now called the 'Adriatic,' but the sea south of Greece and Italy.*"

the writer [T. F.] respectfully requested him to name the authorities which sustained this statement. It caused very great surprise when he merely referred to Horace and Ptolemy!! It was expected he would have named some authority which had been overlooked in the discussion of this subject. As it was otherwise, it is very clear that his note to verse 27

ought not to have been printed. Horace, who was born B.C.
65, or ninety-five years before the Voyage, in no way sanctions
the opinion of Dean Alford.

The passages in Horace naming ADRIA are:—

> 1. "Quamvis nil extra numerum fecisse modumque
> Curas, interdum nugaris ruro paterno.
> Partitur lintres exercitus : *Actia* pugna
> Te duce *per pueros* hostili more refertur.
> Adversarius est frater ; lacus Adria ; donec
> Alterutrum velox Victoria fronde coronet."
>
> *Ad Lollium*, Epist. lib. i. ep. 18, lin. 63.

Mr. Smith (p. 168) cited these lines, and actually added
the words, "Horace places Actium on Adria." He could not
have comprehended that the passage related to the play of
children, in which some part of the sea of Adria represented
the Ambraciot Gulf ; nor does he seem to have been aware
that Horace knew the Adriatic Sea in his voyage to Athens and
a second time on his return from the battle of Philippi (B.C.
42) ; and above all, that he was born in Apulia, near the river
Aufidus, which flows into the Adriatic ("et Adriacas qui ver-
berat Aufidus undas."—*Lucanus*, lib. ii. 404. *Carm.* lib. iii.
carm. 4, l. 10 ; and see *Notes and Queries*, 4th series, April 11,
1868, pp. 336 and 558.) "Egressos sinu Ambracio in *Ionium*,"
are the words of Pliny (lib. iv. ch. 1, p. 189).

> 2. "Ipsum me melior cum peterit Venus,
> Gratâ detinuit compede Myrtale
> Libertina, fretis acrior *Adriæ*
> Curvantis Calabros sinus."—*Carm.* lib. i. carm. 33.

The Calabrian coast was a continuation, on the Adriatic shore,
of the coast of Apulia, and Brundusium was in Calabria, though
the modern name of Calabria includes what was anciently Bruttium. Ancient Calabria was what is now the *Terra di Otranto*.
The Calabria of the ancients was the *heel*, and the Calabria of
our days is the *toe* of Italy.

It is perfectly obvious that the Calabrian coast, which was
washed by the Adria, will not assist the argument in favour of
an African island washed by the Libyan Sea.

3. " Quid bellicosus Cantaber et Scythes,
    Hirpine Quincti, cogitet, *Adriâ*
      Divisus objecto, remittas
        Quærere."

                Ad Hirpinum, Carm. lib. ii. carm. 11.

4. " Quanquam sidere pulchrior
    Ille est : tu levior cortice et improbo
    Iracundior *Adriâ*
      Tecum vivere amem : tecum obeam libens."

                Carm. lib. iii. carm. 9, l. 21.

5. " Frustra cruento Marte carebimus
    Fractisque rauci fluctibus *Adriæ;*
      Frustra per Autumnos nocentem
      Corporibus metuemus, AUSTRUM." [S.]

          Ad Posthumum, Carm. lib. ii. carm. 14.

6.   ". . . neque Auster
    Dux inquieti turbidus *Adriæ.*"

            Carm. lib. iii. carm. 3.

7.   ". . . ego quid sit ater
    Adriæ, novi, sinus; et quid albus
      Peccet Iapyx."

            Carm. lib. iii. carm. 27.

8. " O quantus instat navitis sudor tuis,
    Tibique pallor luteus,
    Et illa non virilis ejaculatio,
      Preces et aversum ad Jovem
    IONIUS udo cum remugiens SINUS
    Noto carinam ruperit."

          Ad Maevium, Epod. lib. carm. 10.

When so respected a divine as the late Very Rev. Dean Alford referred to Horace, it has become important to enable the reader to see how mistaken he was in suggesting that Horace extended the limits of Adria beyond the sea now known under this name. That Mr. Smith should have blundered is not surprising. It is important, however, to have known why Dean Alford entertained the opinion he printed.

Ptolemy, who was born many years after the Voyage—for he was alive A.D. 161, was said by Dean Alford, when describing *a map*, [bk. viii.] to have extended the word " Adriatic " to the sea south of Sicily and of Crete, that is, that he varied from his most precise and distinct words in the preceding book [*ante*, p. 35], especially descriptive of the border seas of Sicily and Crete. His very clear statements respecting the Libyan and African seas, and that Malta was an African island in the African Sea, preclude such an inference. If the MS. map photographed in the photographed copy of the MSS. of Ptolemy, published by Victor Langlois, at Paris, in the year 1867, is to be accepted as part of a reliable MS., no doubt can be entertained, if any map is to be depended on, that Ptolemy consistently held the defined opinions expressed in bk. iii., when the later portions of his work were written; nor do I think the words of bk. viii. to be inconsistent with the distinct statements of bk. iii. There are some words in the MS. map of Langlois relating to the Adriatic, which are not on the engraved map of the folio edition of 1619, but both maps have drawn upon them a sketch of the island of Sicily, which divides the words "Africanon Pelagos," marked on the sea divided by the sketch of this island. But surely Pliny, who was in Italy when St. Paul was there, is the best of guides, and equal in importance are the statements of Pomponius Mela. Their authority, and that of Strabo, Diodorus Siculus, Seneca, and Aulus Gellius, ought to control suggestions opposed to their distinct statements.—T. F.]

OVID.

[Mr. Smith (p. 168) says, " Ovid *repeatedly* calls this sea " Adria," namely, "the sea between Crete and Malta " (p. 158), and he refers to *Fasti*, lib. iv. 501; and *Tristia*, lib. i. Eleg. 12. It cannot be said he was justified in using the word *repeatedly*, or by representing that Ovid has even once expressed this opinion. Ovid was born B.C. 43, or 103 years before the Voyage; but if he gave the name of "Adria " to the expanse of the southern sea, it would most certainly be an important fact. He says:—

> " Effugit et Syrtes et te, Zanclæa Charybdi,
>   Et vos, Nisæi, naufraga monstra, canes ;
> *Hadriacum*que patens late, bimaremque Corinthon.
>   Sic venit ad portus, Attica terra, tuos."
>
> *Fast.* lib. iv. 494.

These words are part of a description of the course of Ceres from the Straits of Messina to Corinth. The tempestuous portion of the Mediterranean is placed by ancient writers off the coast of Macedonia and Epirus. It was and is a locality of storms. Ceres is described to be passing this portion of the sea to Corinth, and the waves of Adria were poetically supposed to extend along the west coast of Greece; but the argument in favour of Malta is necessarily directed to exclude the vessel from this part of the Mediterranean Sea. The course taken did not touch the sea lying between Malta and Crete.

The other passage, cited from Ovid, *Trist.* lib. i. Eleg. 11, lin. 4, is,—

> " Littera quæcunque est toto tibi lecta libello,
>   Est mihi sollicitæ tempore facta viæ.
> Aut hanc me, gelidi tremerem cum mense Decembris
>   Scribentem mediis *Hadria* vidit aquis;
> Aut, postquam bimarem cursu superavimus Isthmon,
>   Alteraque est nostræ sumta carina fugæ."

These words also relate to the same part of the sea referred to in the passage already cited, the stormy character of which Ovid related from his own experience.

When Ovid spoke of the expanse of the sea, he wrote "*Ionium* rapax" (*Fast.* lib. iv. 565). Then, again, he says, "Et maris *Ionii* transieritis aquas" (*Epist. ex Ponto*, lib. iv. Epist. v. ver. 6); and the commentator (edit. Amstel. 1683) adds, "illud est quod Siciliam inter et Græciam patet." And speaking of Malta itself, Ovid wrote:—

> " Fertilis est *Melite*, sterili vicina Cosyræ,
>   Insula, quam *Libyci* verberat unda freti."
>   *Fast.* lib. iii. 568.

And these words clearly and distinctly contradict the statement, that Ovid called the sea between Malta and Crete by the name of "Adria."

The opinions of Mr. Smith, so far as he referred them to the statements of ancient writers, living within 100 years before and 200 years after the Voyage, depended on Horace (p. 158), Ovid (p. 158), born, B.C. 43; Ptolemy, who was alive, A.D. 161; and Pausanias (p. 162), living about A.D. 174.

He does not cite the words of Cicero or of Diodorus Siculus, Why did he not do so? They described the importance of the

island of Malta. Would it not have more than weakened his
argument had he done so? He cites Procopius, living A.D.
527 (p. 159); Orosius, living A.D. 413, who says *Crete* is
bounded on the south by the Libyan *or Adriatic* Sea; and who
also says that *Sicily* is bounded on the east by the Adriatic
Sea, and *on the south by the African Sea*—'a meridie mari
Africo quod est contra Subventanos et Syrtes Minores' (lib. i.
cap. 2, p. 33, ed. Havercamp. Lug. Bat. 1767). He mentions
the southern promontories of Sicily, and as Malta is less than
100 miles immediately south of Sicily, it seems to be an inevitable conclusion that Orosius placed Malta in the African Sea.
In a preceding passage (p. 30) he calls part of the coast sea
from the east to the Lesser Syrtes, the *Sicilian*, or, "*rather
the Adriatic* Sea." But as Orosius lived 350 years after the
Voyage, it is needless to dwell on his opinions. If the African
Sea was, in his day, south of Sicily, how could the sea south
of Malta be called either the Sicilian or the Adriatic Sea?
When he wrote "Libyan *or* Adriatic," was he thinking of the
disputed words before us? Though born in Spain, he was an
African priest. Herodian, who was alive A.D. 238 (lib. viii.
ch. 1, sec. 5) says, ἐν μὲν τοῖς δεξιοῖς [the right] Ἰταλίας μέρεσιν
ἐς τὸ Τυρρηναῖον πέλαγος, ἐν δὲ τοῖς λαιοῖς [on the left] ἐς τὸν
Ἰόνιον κόλπον, and therefore he overrides Orosius.

The reader has now before him what is believed to be a
correct exposition of the grounds on which it is alleged that,
at the time of the Voyage, the term "Adria" described the
sea between Crete and Malta, or between Sicily and Greece,
including in it the island of Malta. Such conclusions appear
to be without foundation.ʸ—T. F.]

ʸ Mr. Smith says (p. 162), " Ptolemy and Pausanias were contemporaries
of Adrian, who was born A.D. 76 (and he might have added, died 10th July,
A.D. 138, aged 62). We do not know the dates of their birth (he adds), but
the *chances* are *two to one* against the supposition that they were both younger
than the Emperor. One of these authors, and it is immaterial which, was
probably born about the time *when St. Luke wrote* [*i.e.* A.D. 60], or very soon
after!" Ptolemy, therefore, if born before the year A.D. 60, would have been
100 years old in A.D. 161, when he was alive, and Pausanias 114 years old
when he was living, A.D. 174, if either were born about the time St. Luke
wrote.—See *Dictionary of Greek and Roman Biography:* "*Hadrianus*" and
"*Pausanias.*"

CONTINUATION OF THE VOYAGE.

Ver. 27. After much tossing about in Adria they apprehended at last that they were approaching "some country" [which "was nearing them"—T. F.], although the darkness of the night did not admit of the truth of their suspicions being ascertained. Ver. 28. They, therefore, sounded repeatedly the depth of the sea, and from the decrease of the depth, from twenty to fifteen fathoms, they judged that their apprehensions were well founded.

Fearing, therefore, that they might fall on the rocks in the darkness of the night, when few or none could escape, they cast Ver. 29. four anchors from the stern of the ship, and waited anxiously for the return of day.

This passage has given occasion to some jocular reflections on this narrative, as anchors are in the present age cast from the prow,[1] not from the stern of the ship. But this is not the Oriental custom. Sir J. Chardin tells us that the modern Oriental caiques, to which he compares the ship of St. Paul, always carry their anchors at the stern, and never at the prow; and these are carried at some distance from the ship by means of the skiff, so as to have an anchor on each side.[2]

---

[1] The anchor was cast from the prow of Roman navigators.

"Anchora de prora jacitur."—*Virgil*, Æn. iii. 277.

[2] [Mr. Smith smiled at this explanation (pp. 131 and 179). He did not deal fairly with the passage, and illustrated from medals, &c., the fact that ancient ships anchored from the prow. Dr. Falconer did not say that such was *not* the case with Roman and Greek ships. He was well versed in numismatic studies, through which illustrations of ancient ships are obtainable, and an important portion of his library related to such studies. He distinctly said in the note, "The anchor was cast from the prow by Roman navigators." It is Sir J. Chardin whom he cites to illustrate an *Oriental* custom of carrying the anchor at the stern. This was blamelessly allowable. Mr. Smith gives a drawing of the prow of an ancient ship, forming a portion of a picture of Theseus deserting Ariadne, and amusingly or absurdly wrote, "A ship so strictly contemporaneous with that of St. Paul, that there is nothing impossible in the supposition that the artist had taken his subject *from that very ship* on loosing from the pier of Puteoli"!! (Page 132.) It would have been equally to the purpose to have suggested that the figure of Theseus represented the captain of the ship!—T. F.]

The mariners of the ship, in their distress, were desirous, in the darkness of the morning of the fourteenth day, to secure themselves by gaining the shore in the boat, and accordingly Ver. 30. lengthened or loosened [b] the rope at the stern, and towed the boat, under colour of casting anchors out of the foreship; and Ibid. probably it was their attempting to do what was so unusual in the navigation of that age and country which caused St. Paul to suspect that they meant to provide for their own safety at the expense of the lives of the other passengers, and, therefore, he said to the centurion and soldiers, " Except these abide in the ship ye cannot be saved."

An observation of Sir J. Chardin should here be mentioned, which is, that the Eastern people do not hoist their boats or skiffs into the ship, but leave them in the water, fastened to, and See ver. 16 of this chapter. towed along by, the stern of the vessel. The taking up of the boat then, and the difficulty of coming by it, mentioned above, does not imply that it was hoisted up into the ship, but it was drawn towards the ship, close to the stern ; and the word which in this place is translated " letting down into the sea," [c] must mean letting out a greater length of rope from the stern, from which the boat was towed ; [d] by which they meant to bring the boat round to the prow of the vessel, which, by being nearer to the land, might facilitate their escape on shore.

The soldiers, and possibly the centurion himself, warned by St. Paul of the intention of the mariners, which so nearly concerned the safety of those who were likely to be thus abandoned, obviated the purpose of the sailors, by cutting asunder the towing-line of the boat, and setting her adrift. Ver. 37.

. The numbers of the people on board are next specified, and amounted, we are told, to 276 persons, a large number, according to modern ideas, for a trading ship of that age to carry.

But Sir John Chardin clears up this difficulty by supposing,

---

[b] *Harmer's Obs.*, vol. ii. p. 496.

[c] Χαλασάντων τὴν σκάφην εἰς θάλασσαν.—V. 30. " The word χαλάω signifies *expando*, as well as *demitto*."—*Schleusner*.

[d] It is usual in the present age for the Egyptian vessels to tow shallops or large boats after them, in their passage down the Red Sea. Niebuhr says that the vessel on board of which he embarked at Suez towed after her three large shallops and one small.

very reasonably, that this Alexandrian ship was like a modern Egyptian saique, of 320 tons burden, and capable of carrying from 24 to 30 guns; and this computation of its size is not at all incredible. Niebuhr describes the vessel in which he took his passage from Suez as being much larger, and able to carry at least forty guns.

But to come nearer to the date of this transaction, Lucian describes [c] an Alexandrian corn-vessel of 180 feet in length, more than 45 feet wide, and 43¼ feet deep. The tonnage of such a ship, according to the usual mode of calculation, would be 1938·6 tons. [f]

Ver. 39.

At this crisis of the voyage, those on board again lightened the ship by casting out the lading of the wheat into the sea; which part of the cargo appears to have been spared when they before threw some of the lading overboard.

When the day came fully on, it appears that they were still ignorant of the place on which they were likely to be stranded; but discovering a small creek with a beach, they purposed to thrust the ship into it, and thereby to facilitate their escape on shore. In consequence of this intention, they weighed their anchors, or cut them off or slipped them, loosed the rudder-bands, hoisted the artemon [g] ["a small fore-sail".—T. F.], and made towards the land.

---

[c] 'Navigium seu Vota.'

[f] According to the English foot; but if measured according to the Roman foot it amounts to 1751 tons. [Mr. Smith properly corrected this estimate. The calculation, founded on the length given by Lucian, is extreme, being more than the length of the keel, which is not given. Reasonably excluding from the length given what may have been more than the length of the keel only, he concludes the tonnage to have been less than 1300 tons.—T. F.]

[g] [The word "artemon" is mistranslated in the Authorised version "main-sail," and the word "main-sail" contradicts the narrative. (V. 19.) It means "a small fore-sail." Wyclif called it "a litil sail." The Latin version has "levato artemone." In White and Riddle's Dictionary it is said to have been "a small sail put upon the mast above the main-sail," citing Jabolenus, Dig. 50, 16, 242, who lived about A.D. 138. Henricus Florez, in his work 'Medallas de las Colonias de España,' Madrid, 1757, gives a copy of a medal of Ibera Ilercanovia (pl. 28, num. 10). It represents a ship with a rudder having the main-sail set; and in front of it, on the prow, a small sail. Mr. Smith has printed illustrations of this fore-sail of ancient vessels. Juvenal (Sat. 12, lib. iv.), only briefly cited by Mr. S.—frightened perhaps by the winds Eurus and Auster (which he omitted from the citation), and his own storm-sails

St. Luke next informs us that, in the attempt to run the ship
aground, they fell into a place where two seas met; [h] by which
we may understand an eddy or surf, which beat on the stern of
the vessel while the head remained fast aground; [i] in which
situation it was to be expected, and indeed it so happened, that
the ship should soon fall to pieces; but the proximity to the
shore, and the assistance afforded by the broken pieces of the
wreck, providentially brought them all safe to land.　　Ver. 44.

When they had reached the shore in safety, they discovered Acts xxviii. 1.
that the island on which they were cast was named MELITE.

MALTA.

It has been a subject of much difference of opinion among the
commentators whether the island here specified was the noted
island of MALTA, on the southern coast of Sicily, formerly called
Melite; or an obscure island in the Adriatic Sea, which was
formerly called by the same name, and which is now known by
the name of MELEDA.

I am of opinion that the island MELEDA, last mentioned, is
the one here alluded to.

---

being forgotten [*ante* 29]—represents a vessel tossed about in a storm, the
throwing overboard of many articles, and finally the cutting down of the main-
mast. Then, the storm lulling: "*fatum valentius et Euro et pelago*":

> ". . . Modica nec multum fortior aura
> Ventus adest: inopi miserabilis arte cucurrit
> Vestibus extentis, et, quod superaverat unum,
> Velo prora suo; jam deficientibus Austris,
> Spes vitæ cum solo redit."—*Juv.* lib. iv. Sat. 12, l. 66.

And the Scholiast adds:

> "Id est, *artemone solo* velificaverunt."—T. F.]

[h] [The words of verse 41 are: περιπεσόντες δὲ εἰς τόπον διθάλασσον ἐπέ-
κειλαν τὴν ναῦν. Mr. Bryant was of opinion that τόπος διθάλασσος described
the natural barrier of a harbour such as a headland, which they endeavoured
to get round, and failed; and he commended the meaning given to the words
by Beza, "une langue de terre entre deux mers."—T. F.]

[i] [The Vatican version omits the words "of the waves." The reading may
mean "by the violence"—*i. e.* of the concussion—the tempest having ceased.
At the southern extremity of Meleda the broad channel of Meleda is on one
side, and the main sea on the other.—T. F.]

My reasons are as follow:

The island of Meleda lies confessedly in the Adriatic Sea; which situation cannot, without much strain on the expression, be ascribed to the island of Malta, as I have before shown.

Meleda lies nearer the mouth of the Adriatic than any other island of that sea, and would, of course, be more likely to receive the wreck of any vessel that should be driven by tempests towards that quarter.

The manner in which MELITE (*Meleda*) is described by St. Luke agrees with the idea of an obscure place, but not with the celebrity of MALTA at that time. Cicero speaks of MELITE (*Malta*) as abounding in curiosities and riches, and affording employment to the weavers of women's garments. Fine linen was made in the island. The Temple of Juno there, which had been preserved inviolate by both the contending parties in the Punic wars, possessed great stores of ivory ornaments, particularly figures of Victory,[k] " antiquo opere et summa arte perfectæ."

[" MELITE," says Cicero, anno B.C. 70, " is an island separated from Sicily by a wide and dangerous sea, with a town in it of the same name. Verres was never in the island, though he employed, for his own purposes during three years, the weavers there of women's garments. On a promontory not far from the town is an ancient Temple of Juno, which, throughout all time, was considered so sacred that it ever remained inviolate and respected, not only during the Punic wars, which were carried on in those parts chiefly by naval forces, but even continued so in the midst of a thieving multitude. It is recorded, moreover, that when the fleet of King Masinissa put in there, the Royal commander removed from the Temple some ivory tusks of an enormous size, carried them to Africa, and presented them to Masinissa. The King, it is said, was at first pleased with the

---

[k] *Oratio in Verrem*, lib. iv. sec. 18 et ch. 46, sec. 103. See Val. Maximus, lib. i. ch. 20. At one time Cicero proposed to himself to retire to Malta : " Mea causa autem alia est, quod beneficio vinctus ingratus esse non possum, nec tamen [*me*] in acie, sed MELITÆ aut alio in loco simile [oppidulo] futurum puto. Nihil, inquies, juvas eum, in quem ingratus esse non vis. Immo nimis fortasse voluisset. Sed de hoc videbimus. Exeamus modo, quod ut meliore tempore possimus, facit ADRIANO MARI Dolabella, Fretensi Curio."—*Epist. ad Atticum*, lib. x. ep. 7, A.U.C. 705 scripta in Cumano.

gift, but, when he had learnt from whence they came, returned
them immediately by a special vessel, and hence the reason for
the inscription on the tusks, in the Punic character, to this
effect :—' *Masinissa received these inconsiderately ; on being
informed of the facts he restored them.'*

" There was there, also, a large store of ivory, carving in ivory,
and figures of Victory in ivory, of ancient and most skilful work-
manship. All, in short everything, this man on a sudden, and
with sudden demand, removed and shipped off by the agency of
servile and thieving collectors despatched for the purpose.
Immortal Gods ! whom do I accuse—whom do I thus judicially
prosecute—what is the character of the man on whom you are
to pass judgment ? This is what the deputies from Melite
say :—' The Temple of Juno has been plundered. In that most
sacred place he has left nothing remaining. Where the fleet of
an enemy often came, where pirates were wont, yearly almost,
to winter—that which no practised robber had ever profaned
and no enemy had ever placed his hands upon, this man singly
has so stripped and spoiled that not a vestige is left.' "][1]

" Malta," says Diodorus Siculus,[m] " is furnished with many and
very good harbours, and the inhabitants are very rich ; for it is
full of all sorts of artificers, among whom there are excellent
weavers of fine linen. Their houses are very stately and beautiful, adorned with graceful eaves, and pargeted with white
plaster. The inhabitants are a colony of Phœnicians, who,
trading as merchants as far as the Western Ocean, resorted to
this place on account of its commodious ports and convenient
situation for a sea trade ; and by the advantage of this place,

---

[1] [In *Verrem*, act ii. lib. iv. 46, 103 : " Dicunt legati Meletenses publice
spoliatum templum esse Junonis : nihil istum in religiosissimo fano reliquisse,
quem in locum classes hostium sæpe accesserint, *ubi piratæ fere quotannis
hiemare solent,* &c." This speech was not delivered : the first oration against
Verres was in August, B.C. 70. The descriptions of Malta given by Cicero and
Diodorus have been tolerably well suppressed by some writers on the Voyage,
and the words used by Cicero have been passed over in the *Life of St. Paul* as
simply " well known." Would they have been suppressed if they had been
thought to favour the arguments on the Maltese side of the question ? Is not
the suppression censurable if it were desired that truthful opinions only should
prevail ?—T. F.]

[m] [Diodor. lib. v. c. 1, Booth's translation. Diodorus is supposed to have
written his work after the year B.C. 8.—T. F.]

the inhabitants presently became famous both for their wealth and merchandise."

[Or, more literally, "The inhabitants are wealthy; workmen of all kinds are found there, but they are especially distinguished for the manufacture of linen garments remarkable for their lightness and softness of texture. There are considerable houses, ambitiously decorated with cornice mouldings, and particularly with stucco-work. The inhabitants are a colony of Phœnicians, who, extending their commerce to the Western Ocean, adopted it as a place of refuge on account of its harbours and its position far from the mainland. The inhabitants profiting in various ways by the presence of traders, rose in their style of living and increased in reputation."] [n]

It is difficult to suppose that a place of this description could be meant by such an expression as " an island called Melite ; " nor could the inhabitants, with any propriety of speech, be understood by the epithet " barbarous." [" If, therefore, I know not the meaning of the speech, I shall be a barbarian to him that speaketh, and he that speaketh will be a barbarian to me."— 1 Cor. xiv. 11. Dean Alford converted the expression into " natives." Its meaning is doubtful, and any conclusion from it may be neglected.—T. F.]

But the Adriatic Melite perfectly corresponds with that description. Though too obscure and insignificant to be particularly noticed by the ancient geographers, the opposite and neighbouring coast of Illyricum is represented by Strabo as agreeing with the expression of St. Paul. [" As in Italy, the climate is warm and the soil productive of fruits—olives, also, and vines grow readily, except in some few very rugged places. Although Illyria possesses these advantages, it was formerly neglected, through ignorance, perhaps, of its fertility; but it was principally avoided on account of the savage manners of the inhabitants and their piratical habits."]

[Cluverius (p. 435) describes, on the authority of Fazellus (alive A.D. 1560), the greatness of the Temples of Juno and Hercules at Malta, the remains of which were extensive. He cites, also, on the subject of these buildings, Fazellus de

---

[n] The two most ancient settlements in Malta appear to have been at Krendi and Bengamma.

rebus Siculis, Quintinus, and Jacomo Bozio (lib. v. par. 3, p. 90).

Mr. Bryant, also, cites an inscription, first mentioned by Gualtherus (*Rerum Sicularum et adjacentium Insul. tabulæ Maltanæ*, 1625), and afterwards by Spon (*Miscell. Erudit. Antiq.* p. 191):

CHRESTION AVGVST. L
PROCVRATOR INSVLARVM
MELIT. ET GAVL.
COLVMNAS CVM FASTIGIIS ET PARIETIBVS
TEMPLI DEAE PROSERPINAE
VETVSTATE RVINAM IMMINENTIBVS (MINITANTIBVS?)
RESTITVIT
SIMVL ET PILAM INAVRAVIT.

Mr. Bryant thus translates the above :—" Chrestion, a freed-man of Augustus, Procurator of the islands of Malta and Gaulos, repaired the pillars, together with the roof and walls of the temple of the goddess Proserpine, which through age were ready to tumble down, and he likewise gilded the ball." The history of Rhodes shows that the military knights of Malta were no respecters of antiquities, and they probably destroyed all ancient monuments at Malta.

An inscription once existed which named a " Protos Meliten-sium " (ch. xxviii. v. 7). It supplied no date. The word Protos, in the plural, is to be found—Luke xix. 40, " the chiefs of the people;" Acts xiii. 50, " the chiefs of the city;" Acts xxviii. 17, " the chiefs of the Jews." That there should not have been a chief man in the island of Meleda is improbable.—T. F.]

[These matters are noticeable :

1. That Ptolemy, who was alive A.D. 161, mentions, as well as Cicero, the " city of Melite," likewise the " temple of Juno," and also adds to these the " temple of Hercules." The temple of the goddess Proserpine was, no doubt, of a much later date. Dio-dorus Siculus, also, describes the prosperous state of the island.

2. The notices of Malta by these writers present an important and unanswerable difficulty : St. Paul departed in a ship of Alexandria which had wintered in the island, whose sign was " Castor and Pollux "—not said to be one of other ships. It was an Alexandrian ship, and its seamen must have known Malta if they wintered there. In what bay or port did they winter, and from whence did they sail ? It was impossible for them to have

wintered in what is called " St. Paul's Bay." The city of Melite was close by, and the safe harbour of Malta was accessible, where even pirates wintered, in order, no doubt, to avoid the winter dangers of the Greek islands. Is it credible that St. Luke, if they parted from the harbour of Melite, or from the neighbourhood of the city of Melite, would simply have said this ship—an Alexandrian ship—"wintered in the isle" [ἐν τῇ νήσῳ]? St. Luke named in the Narrative the towns of Sidon, Myra, Cnidus, Lasea, Phœnîce; but the city of Melite he does not name. They reached and they left " an island," and yet the harbour of Melite was their only place of departure if they were at Malta. The simple word " island" was a perfectly appropriate expression as regarded Meleda, and they arrived at an island " CALLED " Melite: not apparently at an island " et urbs cum portu "—as Scylax describes Malta. The words ὅτι Μελίτη ἡ νῆσος καλεῖται, seem also to express the insignificance of the island.

Mr. Smith, notwithstanding every effort of his imagination, could not give his own testimony to favour what he contended for from anything *he* saw in Malta.

1. What is the present state of the Bay of St. Paul?

Answer, pp. 149 and 166:

" Perhaps there is no surface, of equal extent, in so *artificial* a state as that of Malta is at the present day; and nowhere has the *aboriginal forest* been more completely cleared; but it by no means follows that this was the case when St. Luke wrote."

In a few words, Mr. Smith could not see what would confirm his opinion: the surface is "artificial," and an "aboriginal forest" is gone; but, he said, it was probably there "when St. Paul landed!" A very intelligent friend of mine has sent to me what I have no doubt is a most accurate drawing of the bay. He says, "You will see by the drawing I made on the spot, that the little insignificant passage between the mainland and the Salmonetta Island cannot be called 'a place where *two* seas met;' and 'two seas' would probably mean two appearances of the sea much alike, such as would have been the case had they landed near the end of any island of the sea. The conjecture that Malta was once wooded is, I think, untenable. I have been over the whole island, and I walked from one end of it to the other; a great part is bare rock. On the eastern part of it there are several palm-trees, and here and there a carouba-tree; but the western part would appear to have been in former times altogether uninhabited. I had no companion with me, but had I had one he would have smiled if it had been suggested to him that trees of any kind had flourished there. The single palm-tree that is now seen in the bay is, of course, of recent date, and it is quite on the shore, where it has found sufficient earth for its growth: in the district beyond and around no trees could grow. When I arrived at Malta it had not rained for two years sufficiently to fill the reservoirs. The construction of an enormous tank in the rock, in Città Notabile, was undertaken in consequence of a long drought. The garrison and the inhabitants derived their supplies from the tanks built by the knights, and from those which are constructed underneath the houses. The droughts are of long continuance, and then vegetation languishes."

This ought to dispose of any doubt respecting the supposed existence of an " aboriginal forest" in the time of St. Paul.

A very great authority, also, on Maltese questions, writes thus, " In 1867 the drought was so serious as to create a deficiency of water for the population, except under a restricted allowance from the public tanks and aqueducts, which are both dependent on local rains. I have known two such droughts. In one the shipping had to go to Sicily for water, but now the navy condense their fresh water from the sea as a general practice,.and are thus made independent of a local supply at Malta."

Captain Spratt discovered in the island the fossil remains of a remarkable class of pigmy elephants, of which an adult could not have been larger than a full-grown hog. (See Dr. Hugh Falconer's *Palæontological Memoirs*, vol. ii. p. 292.) Did Mr. Smith's "aboriginal forest" and the existence of these animals cease at the same time? (!) °

° In January, 1870, Dr. A. A. Caruana discovered the bones of fossil elephants in a fissure at Is-Shantin, at the entrance of the quarry of Micabidda, in the island of Malta. " This fissure is said [*Quarterly Journal of the Geological Society*, vol. xxvi. April 13, 1870, p. 435] to raise the number of localities in Malta in which elephant remains have been found in abundance to five, namely, the cave at Casal Zebbug, discovered in 1859 by Captain Spratt; two caves at Tal-Maghlak, in Casal Krendi, discovered by Dr. A. Leith Adams in 1861; the Grandia fissure, within the limits of Micabidda and Casal Siggeni, excavated in 1865 by Dr. Adams and Dr. Caruana; and the Is-Shantin fissure, at the entrance of Casal Micabidda. These localities are all in the *denuded* dis-

Secondly; the next admission of Mr. Smith is a very important one. He says (pp. 173 and 239):

" We *must* not only have a twenty-fathom depth and a fifteen-fathom depth, with such a distance between them to allow their standing on, till they had time to prepare for anchoring with four anchors from the stern; they *must*, at this depth, have had good holding ground, with a creek, with a *sandy* beach to the leeward of their anchorage; and this creek *must* have been in a place where two seas meet. . . . I admit there is no longer a creek having a shore or beach on which a ship could run ashore; but *every* geologist *must know* that it *must* have had one, and that at a period, geologically speaking, from the dip of the beds, by no means remote"!!

" The shore from Salmonetta Island to the Mestara Valley is *now* girt with mural cliffs, where a ship *could not be stranded with safety;* but there is a creek, in this line of cliff, *now without a beach*, but which we *know*, from the form of the land, *must*, at one time, *have had a beach*, which *has been* worn away, in the course of ages, by the wasting action of the sea. The degradation of the lands actually taking place at this point of the sea is proceeding *with more than usual rapidity,* owing to the inclination of the beds and the tendency which large fragments of

---

tricts of the eastern half of the island; and in this direction there is abundant evidence of the existence of many similar ossiferous fissures. From the mode of the occurrence of these bones it is inferred that, at the time of their deposition where we now find them, that part of the island was exposed to the impetuous wash of continuous and rapid currents of fresh water."—" These mammalian remains are of unusual interest, comprising the *Hippopotamus Pentlandi*, an animal about as large as the existing Nile species; the *Elephas melitensis* of Falconer, or Pigmy Maltese Elephant, not more than 4½ feet in height; the still smaller *Elephas Falconeri* of Busk, the average height of which at the withers could not have exceeded 2½ to 3 feet; a new large species, named by Dr. Adams, from the place of its discovery, *Elephas Mnaidræ;* the Gigantic Fossil Dormouse, *Myoxus melitensis,* described by Dr. Falconer to be ' as big in comparison to the living dormouse as the bandicoot rat to a mouse,' and the Hollow-jawed Dormouse, *Myoxus Cartei,* another new species detected by the author. Conspicuous among other vertebrate remains are those of the Gigantic Swan, *Cygnus Falconeri;* another large swan; several other species of land and water birds, at least two species of fresh-water turtles, and a lizard."
—*Nature,* vol. v. No. 119, Feb. 8, 1872, p. 280; a notice of *Notes of a Naturalist in the Nile Valley and Malta,* by Andrew Leith Adams, M.B. [Edinburgh, 1871.]

the rock have to fall over when undermined by the sea. I, therefore, think it is not improbable that *the* beach existed at the time of the shipwreck. *If so,*" &c.

Therefore, this admission is, that the present state of the shore affords no evidence that the vessel could have been stranded in safety where it is alleged to have been stranded.

At page 241, Mr. Smith also says: In that branch of the harbour of Valetta works of art are not found more than six or eight feet below the present bottom of the sea; "*but the deposit there must be much more rapid than in any part of St. Paul's Bay.*" Therefore, it may be inferred the ancient features of the bay are unobliterated or little changed; *i.e.* that what "*must* have been" did not exist in the time of St. Paul. If the bay is changed, any modern soundings to identify it are unimportant; as, indeed, they would be under any circumstances after the lapse of 1812 years.

" When neither the sun nor the stars in many days appeared, and no small tempest lay on us, all hope that we should be saved was taken away." Then St. Paul addressed his companions, and, having exhorted them to be of good cheer, said, "Howbeit, we shall be cast on a certain—'some'—[τινα] island" (v. 26). In the next verse τινα is translated "some."—" When the dark morning of the fourteenth day was come, as they were driven up and down in ['through'] Adria, about midnight the shipmen deemed that they drew near to some [τινα] country" [ὑπενόουν οἱ ναῦται προσάγειν τινὰ αὐτοῖς χώραν.] It is not said, they then first saw or discovered land, but that it was "nearing them." If they were in the Adriatic, where even Ptolemy places Meleda, Alexandrian seamen must have known the coast to abound with islands. That on *some* one of the islands they might be wrecked was probable.

They were approaching some country [regio]. Προσάγειν is to move towards, and it seemed "some country was nearing them." This being written by St. Luke, necessarily after the event, he selected the word χώρα. Mr. Smith (p. 118) saw the difficulty suggested by the expression when he said, "The word χώραν evidently means land distinguished from the sea." But St. Luke wrote accurately. If the word means something more than νῆσος, the argument that Malta was the scene of the shipwreck is at an end, for there there is no mainland to be seen distinct from the island. Malta, if reached, would only be *afterwards* correctly described as an island, and the word χώρα would not have been the expression so accurate a writer as St. Luke could be expected to have applied to it. He used this word after he knew they ha'l been wrecked on an island. Darkness had not prevailed all the time of the storm, for the words are, "in many days," that is, several of the fourteen days, neither sun nor stars appeared (v. 20), but when the fourteenth day had come they drew near to "*some*" country [χώρα]. When it was day they knew not the land [γῆν] (v. 39). Then they fell "into a place where two seas met" (v. 41), and if it were Meleda they would have had the broad canal of Meleda on one side and the expanse of the Adriatic on the other. "When they escaped they—'we'—knew the island [νῆσος, not χώρα] was called Melite" (xxviii. 1). At a distance—applying the words of the Dean of Chester used in reference to Salamis—"the view of the island might not have been disentangled from the coast." Meleda is a very woody island.

The word προσάγειν is expressive of the ship drifting on the swell and the current of the sea. It is not what St. Luke, when he wrote, knew to have been an island which was thought to be "nearing them," but that "some country" (regio) was "nearing them," which they once believed to have been only such. And the expression is consistent with their having seen, and being aware they were coming to, the coast of some country, but what region or what particular country "was nearing them" was unknown. The use of anchors would have been needed in consequence of the known force of the current and the swell, after a storm, in the Adriatic Sea.

They chose their place of landing. At first (v. 29) "they were fearful lest they should fall into dangerous or rocky places" [φοβούμενοί τε μήπω κατὰ τραχεῖς τόπους ἐκπέσωμεν]. As the vessel was deliberately stranded, it appears to be a fair inference that there were only the swell usual in this part of the sea after a storm, and the current [said to move ordinarily about a mile an hour] which moved the vessel towards land. The seamen were accustomed to strand vessels, and when they wished to thrust this vessel into some creek, it is not to be inferred they designed to wreck it, or that, in the midst of or after a storm and at anchor, they abandoned their anchors and deliberately drove the vessel among breakers, after having selected their place of landing! They observed a certain creek with a beach, into which they determined, if possible, to run the ship [κόλπον δέ τινα κατενόουν ἔχοντα αἰγιαλόν, εἰς ὃν ἐβουλεύοντο, εἰ δύναιντο, ἐξῶσαι τὸ πλοῖον, v. 39]. These words especially show that the storm had abated, for, if it had not, they could not have expected to have beached the ship in safety; nor could they have expected, having the power to choose the place into which to have thrust the ship, that it would have so struck the shore as to have fallen to pieces. If the storm had not passed it would have been otherwise, and the anchors would not have been slipped. The words "of the waves" [v. 41] are not in the Vatican version, but little or no importance is to be attached to this fact.

May we not, then, reasonably conjecture, in addition to what the narrative expressly states, that land had been seen when St. Paul addressed his companions, for he first alludes to the harm and loss caused by leaving Crete, and then assures them that every man's life shall be safe—as if there were something before them suggesting this assurance—ending with the statement that they should be wrecked on *some* (not "a certain") island [νῆσος], and the word "some" implies one of several islands, which the word "certain" does not. On the fourteenth day they drew near to "*some*" country [χώρα]. If it is clearly established —and it seems to be beyond all doubt—that the expanse of the Mediterranean Sea, according to the authority of all writers contemporary with St. Luke, was not called "Adria," and that the term "Adria" meant what we now call the "Adriatic," the high land of the Illyrian coast must have been distinctly visible before and when the storm abated, and necessarily afterwards when they must have been approaching the island Meleda. The number of men who landed would have enabled them to command the island, and the events of the three months they wintered at Meleda (Melite Adriatica) would have been monotonous, though the Castor and Pollux also wintered there, and there would have been nothing to record. What would have been their position if they had been in or near the city of Malta (Melite Africana)? Is it probable there would have been no occurrence to relate as having happened in three months?

At all events, the words, that "some country" was "nearing

them," represent "drifting" by a current. They do not represent the ship to be then *driven* by the force of the storm towards the land. No current could have carried the vessel, coming from the east towards St. Paul's Bay at Malta, for no current there runs in this direction to the bay from the east. If this meaning of the words, "nearing them," is correct, this other conclusion is a necessary one, namely, that they were at Meleda, where only there could have been such a current as could have drifted them towards land. There is nothing in the Narrative opposed to this conclusion. On the contrary, the Narrative favours it.

It is frequently assumed that they did not see the coast because no mention is made of the Dalmatian mountains; but the very form and matter of the Narrative preclude our requiring any such notice. We are not authorised to conclude that the mountains were unseen; on the contrary, as they were in Adria, they must have been seen.[p] When St. Luke mentioned Cnidus, he was silent respecting the scenery of the lofty mountains of Cape Krio. At this time they were ἐν τῷ Ἀδρίᾳ. These are also the words of Ptolemy (*ante*, p. 56), when speaking of the Gulf only of the Adriatic, and the words so used by Ptolemy are unconnected by the word "sea," or with the name of any border sea. If, also, they were in the Adriatic, χώρα was a correct word to have used.—T. F.]

MELEDA.

[It has been denied that the vessel could have been driven to Meleda. The passage from Horace "*ille Notis actus ad Oricum*" (*ante*, p. 25), has already been cited. A similar case was that of Mr. Galt (*ante*, p. 28), who, leaving Malta in a polacca, intended to reach Spezzia, some 424 miles in a straight line east of

---

[p] [Mr. G. Long, in his *History of the Decline of the Roman Empire*, vol. iv. p. 4, gives a remarkable instance of the brevity of ancient writers. Cæsar mentions his journey from Geneva to Italy, and his return over the mountains with new troops and their arrival in the territory of the Segusiani, in eleven lines!—*Bell. Gall.* i. 10. My admiration of Mr. Long's work can be best expressed in the words of a writer in the 'Saturday Review':—"*Incorrupta fides, nudaque veritas*,—indefatigable research, impartiality worthy of stoic of the strictest sort, and learning abundant and accurate."

Malta, and only 1° 21' north of Malta, was driven to Avlona for refuge in the direction of the wind, in latitude 40° 27' N., being 353 geographical or about 400 English miles northward of Malta, and obtained shelter in Adria. Procopius [q] (*De Bello Gothico*, lib. iii. 40) relates the following as the effect of a storm which occurred about the year A.D. 510, on a fleet sailing from the Adriatic or eastern side of the Mediterranean to Sicily: "Not long afterwards Artabanes was in Cephalonia, and when he heard that Liberius had left and had sailed to Sicily, he also left, and immediately crossed the sea [πέλαγος] called the Adriatic. When approaching Calabria (no doubt in coasting) an extraordinary storm came on, accompanied by wind of fearful violence, *proceeding from a direction contrary to their course.* It caused such a dispersion of the whole fleet as to suggest the possibility of the greater part being carried to the coast of Calabria, and into the power of the enemy. This, however, did not happen, for some of the ships were forced, by the over-whelming violence of the wind, to retrace their course, and to return to the Peloponnesus. Of the remainder some were lost, some saved. One ship, however, on board of which was Artabanes, was in great danger from the loss of the mast which had been broken off by the rolling of the sea, but carried onwards by the tempest-stream (ῥόθιος), and yielding to the violence of the waves, it came to the island MELITE." Liddell and Scott translate ῥόθιος as "rushing of the stream," or "any rushing motion." Calabria is on the south of Italy, and on the east side it is washed by the Adriatic, where, also, is the port of Brundusium (Brindisi). They feared being driven on the southern part of the coast; they had lost their mast, were at the mercy of the waves, and were carried to *Meleda*, or 246 miles to the north of Cephalonia. The word "Adriatic" is used in the above account in reference to what had been called the Ionian Gulf; but as the storm occurred 450 years after the Voyage of St. Paul, this is unimportant; and the word πέλαγος represents a border sea.

---

[q] The writer of the article in the *Dictionary of Geography* is certainly mistaken in the inference he draws from the passages in Procopius cited by him (*Bell. Goth.* i. 15, iii. 40, iv. 6; *Bell. Vand.* i. 13, 14, 23). The most important is that in *Bell. Goth.* iii. 40, quoted above; and by citing it, in reference to Malta, it is evident he misunderstood it. The passage *Bell. Vand.* i. 14, is the same as that referred to, *ante,* p. 62.

The word θάλασσα is not used. It is, also, in this instance observable, that the name "Adriatic" is here given to that part of the sea between Calabria and north of Cephalonia, which the vessel of St. Paul is alleged not to have sailed over, and into which part of the Mediterranean the Adriatic Sea was supposed to discharge itself.

There is, also, another instance of a vessel driven from the Mediterranean Sea into the Adriatic Gulf by a storm, and there wrecked, which must not be disregarded, for it must at one time have attracted the attention of Europe. Richard Cœur de Lion, on leaving Syria, sent his wife, his widowed sister, and family before him, and he himself followed in a fast-sailing vessel. (*History of William of Newburgh*, translation by Rev. Joseph Stevenson, book iv. ch. 31, p. 605, 1856.) The Queen, and those who sailed with her, arrived, after a slow but prosperous course, at Sicily, and continued there in safety for a season under the care of King Tancred; but the vessel which carried Richard encountered a severe storm, and was driven to the north. The King, it is said, suffered shipwreck between Aquileia and Venice, and, with a few followers, scarcely escaped being drowned. "He was made captive by the Duke of Austria, in the month of *December*, in the year 1192, and was kept in chains, without any respect to his Royal dignity." Thus the vessel was driven back or out of its course towards Sicily into Adria, and was there wrecked. It is related that the vessel was wrecked on the island of "Chroma," opposite to Ragusa (A. A. Paton's *Adriatic Islands*, 1849, vol. i. p. 115.)[r] This island, as well as Meleda, was a dependency of Ragusa, and Chroma is not far from the south-east end of Meleda. The Adriatic tradition, therefore, represents Richard Cœur de Lion to have been shipwrecked not far from the scene of the shipwreck of St. Paul;

---

[r] ["Opposite to this Val di Breno road is the little island of La Chroma, which has been taken by the Archduke Maximilian (the unfortunate Emperor of Mexico) for a winter residence. There some of our kind friends took us one evening to a pleasant *fête champêtre*. Most of the island is covered with a beautiful pine wood, fitted up underneath with aromatic shrubs—*agnus castus*, myrtle, box, &c. The garden is really interesting as a collection of plants from every part of the world, successfully acclimatised together, and in a few years it will be beautiful."—*The Eastern Shores of the Adriatic in* 1863, by Viscountess Strangford.]

but the material fact is that the vessel—turned back from its course to Sicily—was unquestionably driven into and wrecked in the Adriatic Gulf.

The place of the landing of Richard I. is illustrated, also, in Sir J. Gardner Wilkinson's work *On Dalmatia and Montenegro*, vol. i. p. 299, 1848. It appears that Richard, on his return from Palestine, having been overtaken by a severe storm after leaving Corfu, made a vow that he would build a church to the Virgin on whatever spot he should first land at, and that having reached the island of Lacroma he made preparations to fulfil his promise. He was afterwards induced to alter his vow, under a dispensation, and to found a church in Ragusa, the Republic undertaking to found another at Lacroma. This church, or cathedral, at Ragusa, was destroyed by the great earthquake of 1667. The Emperor Henry, when he stated in his letter to Philip of France that Richard " had been wrecked near Istria, between Aquileia and Venice," was evidently misled by a vague report which confounded his landing there, *after* his departure from Ragusa, with his previous escape from shipwreck. And Sir J. Gardner Wilkinson further adds, " The account of Richard's arrival at the Isle of Lacroma is highly satisfactory, as it clears up a disputed point and explains the statement of Hoveden, who calls the place of his landing ' Gazere apud Ragusa,' and that there is little doubt the word *'gazere'* is Arabic, meaning *'island,'* and had been adopted, like many other words, by the Crusaders." Sir G. Wilkinson cites *Appendini*, vol. i. p. 272; *Luccari*, lib. i.; *Farlati*, vol. vi. p. 90; and *Von Engel, Hist. Ragusa*, p. 87.—T. F.]

[The late Rev. J. M. Neale, Warden of Sackville College, (*Notes on Dalmatia*, p. 161) expressed his " entire certainty that ' Melita' is Meleda." He further stated " that there is no creek in Malta, such as is described; and in Meleda ' St. Paul's Bay ' answers precisely, and that any Maltese tradition may be repulsed by the universal tradition of the Adriatic in favour of Meleda." And he suggests this case as regards the " drifting " (for a continuous N.E. wind, as Mr. Smith suggests, would have blown the sail-less vessel, in the course of 477 miles, far south of Malta), " that when the ship was in 22° E. long. and 35° N. lat., the wind shifted, *as it so often does,* to E.S.E. The course would then be *directly straight to Meleda ;* no island approaching the line, St. Paul's Bay—the creek so exactly answering the description—would be the first land they would make. On this hypothesis there was not *one single island*, instead of Admiral Penrose's '*so many*,' to pass." The Rev. J. M. Neale further added, "It is said that the sea between Malta and Crete was anciently called ' Adria.' Let us first have a proof of this : as yet I have seen none, except when the word is used vaguely, *e. g.* as one might now say, ' I went from Trieste, by the Adriatic, to Malta ;' which would not mean that the Adriatic reached Malta." Sailing "from the Adriatic to the Tyrrhene," is a similar illustration. But the statement of the Rev. Mr. Neale is condemned as nautically inaccurate in the terms of his proposition. His meaning substantially is, that there is not that difficulty in passing from the Mediterranean to Meleda which has been suggested. Admiral Penrose had said, "that to have drifted *up the Adriatic* to the island of Melite, or Meleda, in the requisite curve, and to have passed so many islands and other dangers in the route, *would, humanly speaking, have been impossible.*" The Rev. Mr. Neale, with imperfect particularity, represented that a vessel in the expanse of the sea might have been so driven. The instances of Artabanes and Richard I., and even of Mr. Galt, show that he was not mistaken.

The Viscountess Strangford—a lady unquestionably of great ability and intelligence—in her work *On the Eastern Shores of the Adriatic in* 1863 [p. 216], says :—

1. " That it is impossible to imagine, for an instant, the ship could have passed up the narrow way between the coast of Otranto and the Akro-Ceraunian mountains without seeing land, or that any vicinity to the latter coast, so much dreaded by ancient and modern navigators, should have been passed over in silence."

Answer.—There is no reason to infer they did not see the mountains. They were in a storm ; they were in Adria. There is silence respecting all that passed, except at the beginning and end of the voyage.

2. " What should a ship of Alexandria have been doing at Meleda, or so far up the Adriatic Sea—a sea which, in those days, led to nothing ? "

Answer.—They were in the Adriatic against their will, and important ports existed in that sea long before the Voyage, though they sought for none of them.

3. "That it is impossible to account for the entire silence which ensues upon so long a voyage as the subsequent one between this island (Meleda) and Rhegium, in which so many various coasts and islands would have been passed."

Answer.—Similar remarks may be made respecting the early part of the Voyage before Crete was reached. But the silence observed respecting Malta (if they reached that island) where they remained for three months, is still more remarkable—so remarkable that it is improbable they were there. But a similar silence to that commented on was observed by Josephus and the writer who relates the voyage of St. Ignatius.—T. F.]

MELEDA.

[And now we reach important evidence, unknown to all early writers and only known to us in recent times, which seems distinctly to confirm the argument in favour of Meleda. It is related in the *Adriatic Pilot,* published by the Hydrographic Office, Admiralty, in 1861, "that past Saseno Island the main stream of the sea appears to divide into two parts. One branch from Cape Linguetta (p. 16) *is generally in the direction of Meleda Island,* with a velocity varying in calm weather from half a knot to two knots (two miles) an hour. When influenced by south-westerly winds, and even in calms, this current frequently sets north-eastward at about three-quarters of a knot." In a note it is added, "that the *Psyche,* French frigate, in a calm here, was carried thirty miles to the north-east in twenty-four hours. . . . Between Cape Linguetta and Meleda southing in the currents is rarely found, and it is only met with on going westward of this line, when it increases as the coast of Italy is approached, especially with a northern breeze. . . . In Meleda channel, with the wind blowing hard from the south-east, the current runs west-north-west at the rate of three or four knots" (pp. 16, 17).

We have in this statement the explanation of the cause of the shipwreck of Richard Cœur de Lion on the island of La Chroma, and of Artabanes being carried to Meleda. If St. Paul were in Adria, where would the ship, in all probability, when driven through Adria, have been wrecked? Most assuredly on or near the island of Meleda. The current of the sea at Malta sets from the west to the east, and therefore could not have aided a vessel drifting to the west from Crete; but the northerly current of the Adriatic, or the current from the Ionian κόλπος, in its usual and ordinary course, would have taken the vessel to the very island when the storm ended. The name of Meleda is no error, and that the ship was in Adria—that is, in the Adriatic—thus ceases to be a doubtful fact in connection with the negative evidence respecting Malta, and the positive and unanimous contemporary evidence of the meaning of the word " Adria." The storm ended in Adria, and the unvarying current of Adria in the direction of Meleda discloses to us that St. Luke did not use the word in a different sense from its use by all those whose writings, while he lived, have been preserved to this day.

We know but little of Meleda Island, and few travellers have visited it. In 1794 Mr. Watkins stated, that " when at Ragusa he went with a party to Meleda, where St. Paul was shipwrecked. An honest monk conducted them to the spot where he landed, still known by the two seas which meet there. The island is held in high veneration by the Ragusans." [s]—*Travels*, vol. ii. p. 312.

The following is the account given of the Mediterranean end of the island in the *Portolano del Mare Adriatico*, Milano, 1830, pp. 407, 408 :—

" The coast trends in an E.S.E. direction for three miles as far as the cape called Cima di Meleda. In this stretch there is no bay of consequence, nor any danger except some reefs awash near the shore in a cove a mile and a half from P. Camera, in which boats belonging to the town of Coritta anchor, which town is a quarter of an hour inland to the southward.

" From point Cima the coast runs S.W. half a mile, then bending S.E. to Point Grui for a mile. Parallel with the first-named portion there is a rock, rugged on the outer side, and 400 paces in length, which forms with the shore a channel,

---

[s] [The Rev. John Eadie, D.D., in his *Biblical Cyclopædia*, 12th edition, p. 433, London, 1870, published by the Religious Tract Society, states that " Malta has an unbroken tradition in its favour." The Rev. David Brown, in vol. vi. of the BIBLE, published by Collins and Co., of Glasgow, 1870 (*Acts*, ch. xxvii.) cites with approval the additions made by Mr. Smith to the Narrative of St. Luke.]

sometimes called Port Cima di Meleda. Its width is not more than half a gomena.[*] It is capable of sheltering small boats, which must, however, not neglect the usual precautions during the continuance of the Bora, because when this wind blows down the channel it causes a heavy sea. They will lie quietly with any other wind. The best place to anchor is near the S.W. entrance, mooring with hawsers to each shore. But the other entrance is the best, beyond question, for getting the vessels into port, on account of a small rock which divides the channel into two narrow passages, so that the western passage has 30 feet of water and the eastern only 10. Within, the bottom is mud and sand, with 20 to 25 feet of water from N.E. to S.W.

"The external coast of Meleda is composed, for the most part, of the *débris* of the island itself. Beyond P. Grui there is a small rocky cove first, and then, after a sweep of about a mile, comes Port Sablonara, the only shelter, and that not good, on the southern part of the island. It is about 1000 yards long from S.W. to E.N.E., 400 paces wide at its entrance, and half that at the other end; 30 to 60 feet deep, bottom sandy. It is capable of accommodating vessels not larger than brigantines, which, however, must take special care not to be caught by S.W. winds."

There are three engravings of the coast outline of the island of Meleda and of the mountains on its northern side (the island lying E.N.E. in Tavola V. of the fine maps of the Adriatic, pub-

---

[*] [The "gomena" is about 200 yards. Whether or not a bay now exists on the coast of the island of Meleda, having at this time, and after the lapse of eighteen hundred and twelve years [1872 – 60 = 1812] a sounding of fifteen fathoms, is a consideration of no importance, and especially if, as is believed, the meaning of the word "Adria," at the time of the Voyage, is indisputably established. And surely, whatever beach existed at that distance of time must have been affected by the operation of earthquakes, which are known to have prevailed on the coast, and especially at Ragusa—not by assuming that the land or rocks of the island of Meleda have suffered any material change but the inevitable accompaniment of "the earthquake wave," must have acted on the shore of the island. Strabo (lib. i.) gives remarkable instances of the effect of that wave. On the western side of South America this wave is always greatly feared. At Lisbon, Nov. 1, 1755, its effect was terribly destructive. Francis Edmunds, Esq., of Wosborough Hall, Yorkshire, the brother-in-law of Dr. William Falconer, was in Lisbon during this earthquake, and I myself spoke to him in 1824 about this event. He was born in 1738, and died in 1825.—T. F.]

lished at Milan). The index map shows that a wind S.E. off Otranto, at the mouth of the Adriatic, would blow directly on the island of Meleda. Foglio XI. of the same maps gives an outline of the island and of soundings with a scale of English fathoms compared with those of other countries.

It is said in the *Italian Pilot*, "Though in former times the island of Meleda of the ancients, according to the opinion of many, was well inhabited and possessed a city, yet, at present, only six small villages are to be seen. A great part of the surface is desert, uncultivated, and full of woods; even the cultivated parts are only moderately fertile. . . . The channel which bears the same name separates it from the peninsula of Sabioncello. Towards the south-west the sea is open. . . . In the interior are many wooded heights, which, at a certain distance towards the south, resemble so many islands. . . . The inhabitants, who are few in proportion to the size of the island, make their largest gains from firewood, which is sent to Ragusa, and from wood for shipbuilding, which is employed in the yards of Curzola and Gravosa."

At an early period it was named as one of four fertile islands: "Habent quoque Pagani in propinquo insulas quatuor, Meletam (Meleda), Curcuram (*Corcyra Nigra*), Bartzum (Brachia) et Pharum (Phara), omnes pulcherrimas fertilissimasque; oppida item deserta et paludes multas, in quibus habitant et jumenta alunt et victum parant."—*Constantinus Porph. de Administrand. Imperio*, vol. iii. p. 146, ch. 30. Bonnæ, 1840.

In the Itinerary of Antoninus [*Bertii*, ed. 1619, p. 33], we have, between Sicily and Africa, the island "Melita," and between Dalmatia and Istria "Melita; a Melita Epidauros, *stadiæ* c. c."

The Emperor Augustus must have almost depopulated the island by the grievous punishment he inflicted on its inhabitants. "Others who had revolted, and inhabited the islands Melite and Corcyra, Augustus swept utterly away on account of their habitual piracy: those who had attained the age of manhood were put to death, and the rest were sold into slavery."—*Appian de Rebus Illyricis*, ch. 16.

It is said, "That from Meleda it would have been more natural to have gone to Brundusium or Ancona, and from thence by land to Rome, rather than to have gone by sea to Puteoli." The conclusion is rather the other way. If the ship were at

Malta, what prevented its making the short passage to Syracuse
in the winter? Brundusium, or Ancona, would have been most
inconvenient ports to have landed a cargo of wheat consigned
to Puteoli, or to be carried to Rome. Even St. Ignatius was not
taken from Dyrrachium to either of these ports, but by sea past
Puteoli.—T. F.]

The circumstance of the viper, or poisonous snake, that fastened
on St. Paul's hand, merits consideration.

Father Giorgi, an ecclesiastic of Melite Adriatica, who has
written on this subject, suggests, very properly, that as there are
now no serpents in Malta, and as it should seem were none in
the time of Pliny, there never were any there, the country
being dry and rocky, and not affording shelter or proper nourish-
ment for animals of that description. But Meleda abounds with
these reptiles, being woody and damp, and favourable to their
way of life and propagation.[u]

The disease with which the father of Publius was affected
(dysentery, combined with fever,[x] probably intermittent) affords
a presumptive evidence of the nature of the island. Such a
place as Melite Africana (Malta), dry and rocky, and remarkably
healthy, was not likely to produce such a disease, which is
almost peculiar to moist situations and stagnant waters,[y] but
might well suit a country woody and damp, and, probably for
want of draining, exposed to the putrid effluvia of confined
moisture.[z]

---

[u] [Mr. Smith (pp. 148–165) suggested that the Fauna of Malta had changed.
Capt. Spratt (*Crete*, vol. ii. p. 7) states that there are no venomous reptiles in
Crete. "Mox Gaulos et Gelata, cujus terra scorpiones, dirum animal Africæ,
necat."—*Plin.* lib. v. ch. 7.

> "Serpentum tellus (Sardinia) pura ac viduata veneno
> Sed tristia cœlo et multa vitiata palude."
> *Silius Rhodig.* ch. 16.—T. F.]

[x] Πυρετοῖς καὶ δυσεντερία συνεχόμενον.
[y] See *Pringle's Diseases of the Army*, passim.
[z] [Mr. Smith says that he was informed by Dr. Galland, of Valetta, that
"dysentery combined with fever" is "by no means uncommon in Malta."
The information should be more precise, for "the peculiarity of the disease to
moist situations" was not stated carelessly, nor can the authority of that most
eminent physician, Sir John Pringle, be so summarily set aside. Is the disease
common or known out of the city of Valetta, and among persons habitually

DEPARTURE FROM MELEDA.

After a stay here of full three months, they departed in a ship of Alexandria, whose sign was "Castor and Pollux,"[a] which,

resident in the island? I have seen forms of severe fever exhibited, in healthy places, by strangers, which were unknown to residents; by persons who, after long sickness, had become barometers of disease on mere changes of weather. The hospital books at Malta would show "whether the disease is by no means uncommon" among the islanders. The report of an English physician, uninterested in local traditions, might be relied on, and it should be kept free from cases where there have been sudden changes of diet at the end of a voyage, or sudden changes to hot in-door life after long out-door exposure.—T. F.]

[a] "Phaselus ille, quem videtis, hospites,
    Ait fuisse navium celerrimus."

"Strangers! the bark you see is fain to say,
  She was the fastest sailer of her day;
  There was no boat, however great its speed,
  But she outstripped it and could take the lead,
  Whether the breeze her yielding canvas swelled,
  Or flashing oars her onward course propelled:
  This is well known to Adria's boisterous seas,
  To Rhodes' fair isle and to the Cyclades,
  Nor yet denied by Thracia's uncouth boors,
  Nor where the Euxine chafes its waveworn stores.
  Where afterwards a boat crewhile she stood,
  The pride and glory of the leafy wood;
  For on Cytorus' lofty crags she grew,
  Her leaflets whispering as the wild winds blew.
  Oh, thou Amastris for thy port renowned,
  And thou, Cytorus, with thy box-trees crowned.
  The truth of what I say full well ye know,
  For on your ridges I was wont to grow—
  Nursed on my native hills in stately pride,
  There was I launched upon thy streams to glide;
  And steering then to many an unknown shore,
  My master through tempestuous seas I bore,—
  Whatever way the winds might chance to blow,
  Or on the starboard or the larboard bow,
  Or whether, by the power of Jove confined,
  Each on the stern its gathered force combined.
  To River Gods she had no offering paid,
  Since her last trip across the seas she made,
  And reached this lake upon whose tranquil breast,
  Old and worn-out she hopes in peace to rest,—

perhaps from similar stress of weather, had wintered in the isle, and came from thence to Syracuse.

If we suppose that St. Paul, with his company, arrived at Meleda about the beginning of December, a stay of three months, and of perhaps something more, will bring their departure from this island to the beginning of March, the tenth day of which month was, according to Vegetius, the time of the commencement of the navigation of merchant ships, and thence called *Natalis Navigationis*.[b] This is about the time of the cosmical rise of Orion,[c] and the putting forth of the leaves of the fig-tree,[d] according to Theophrastus, at which time Hesiod[e] declares navigation to be safe.

The Natalis Navigationis in Egypt, called also Isidis Navigium,[f] was on the third of the nones of March, or on the fifth day of that month; Isis being the representative of the moon, and that planet being supposed to have a great influence on the

---

But dedicates herself to you who reign,
Twin constellations o'er the troubled main."
Ex Catullo, Dedicatio Phaseli.

These lines of Catullus, in which is contained the dedication of a pinnace to the constellation of Castor and Pollux, whose influence upon the sea of Adria is a frequent subject of allusion in the Latin poets, have a peculiar interest, as they throw light upon that apparently trifling, but really important, notice of the ship in which St. Paul was wrecked " whose sign was Castor and Pollux."

" . . . Séque dedicat tibi
Gemelle Castor, et gemelle Castoris."
The Press, Feb. 1872.

Catullus was alive b.c. 47, and his words

" Et hoc negat *minacis* Adriatici
Negare litus,"

certainly do not apply to the Mediterranean, or what was called the Ionian sea.

[b] Veget. lib. iv. c. 29.
[c] " Orion rises cosmically, March 16."—*Plin.* xviii. 26.
[d] " Fig-tree, ἐρινεὸς, leafs 14 Pisces, March 2."—*Theophrastus.*
" Fig-tree, συκή, leafs 29 Pisces, March 17, πρὸ ἰσημερίας δὲ μικρόν."—*Ib.*
" N.B. The vernal equinox, or entrance of the sun into Aries, is placed by Geminus at March 19."—*Petavii Uranologion.*
[e] Οἴγεται ἄρτι θάλασσα ἐφοπλίζοιτε δὲ νῆας
Ὠρίων ἀκλύστων ἄγειν λιμένων.—*Greek Epigram.*
[f] Calend. Constantini Magni, a.d. 325.—*Petavii Uranologion,* p. 112.
Calendaria duo vetusta, quorum in Grutero reperiunda exemplaria.

H

weather,[g] was likely to be introduced as the protectress of navigation.

Lucian and others speak of the moon as having the power to raise or to compose tempests [h] at her pleasure. A writer in the *Theological Repository* [i] has brought an argument in favour of the opinion that the island here in question was the island of Malta, "from," as it is expressed, "St. Paul's calling at Syracuse, in his way to Rhegium, which is, he says, so far out of the track, that no example can be produced in the history of navigation of any ship going so far out of her course, except it was driven by a violent tempest." This argument tends principally to show that the author had a very incorrect idea of the relative situation of the places to which he refers. The ship which carried St. Paul from the Adriatic Sea to Rhegium, would not deviate from its course more than half a day's sail by touching at Syracuse; and the delay so occasioned would probably be but a few hours more than it would have been had they proceeded to Syracuse in their way to the Straits of Messina from Malta, as the map will show. Besides, the master of the ship might have, and probably had, some business at Syracuse, which had originated at Alexandria, from which place it must have been originally intended the ship should commence her voyage to Puteoli, or it needed supplies after its detention during the winter; and in this course the *calling at Syracuse* would have been the smallest deviation possible. The difference, then, on which this writer places so much dependence, is too insignificant to merit further notice.

Again, supposing the ship to have come from Malta, it must have been on account of some business, probably commercial, that they touched at Syracuse in their way to Puteoli, as Malta is scarcely more than one day and night's sail from Syracuse; [k] whereas there might be some reasons respecting the prosecution of the voyage had the ship come from Meleda, which is more than five times that distance,[l] and probably a more uncertain navigation.

Ver. 12.

---

[g] See Long's *Astronomy on the Metonic Cycle*, vol. ii. sec. 1333.
[h] Jablonski, *Pantheon Ægyptiacum*, lib. iii. cap. i. sec. 6.
[i] *Theological Repository*, vol. iv.
[k] Malta is seventy-eight nautical miles, or ninety English miles, from Syracuse.
[l] Meleda is distant from Syracuse 350 nautical miles, or 403 English, in a

After three days' stay at Syracuse, they sailed for the Straits ^{Ver. 12.} of Messina, "and from thence we fetched a compass and came ^{Ver. 13.} to Rhegium," [m] and after, as it should seem, one day's stay at Rhegium, the south wind blew and brought them on the ensuing day to Puteoli. This must be understood as a voyage of two days' sail, as the distance is near 1900 stadia, or more than the extent of three degrees of latitude, which, with a fair wind, as it seems they had, might be performed in two days and a night.

Thucydides, [n] speaking of the usual computation of sailing, says that a ship will pass from Naples to Sicily in two days and a night. Now, Naples is close upon Puteoli, and Rhegium lies on the strait that divides Sicily from Italy. A fair wind, as in the present instance, might accelerate the voyage a little above the usual calculation.

[On the sailing of ancient ships, Mr. Smith (p. 209) has an important note, viz., " Pliny tells us that the prefects Galerius and Babilius made quick passages from the Straits of Messina to Alexandria; the former arrived on the seventh and the latter on the sixth day. That in the following summer Valerius Marianus made this passage from Puteoli on the ninth day ' lenissimo flatu.' Pliny also mentions passages from the Straits of Hercules to Ostia in seven days; from the nearest port in Spain in four; from the province of Narbonne in three; and from Africa in two (*Plinii Nat. Hist.* lib. xix. *Prœm. ed. Lug. Bat.* 1668, p. 527)." Mr. Smith further added, " Upon these passages Admiral Beechy offers the following remarks : ' It does not appear that there is any mistake in the numbers here mentioned by Pliny; for the instances are all of them consistent with each other, one being below 140 M.P. per day, and another 143 M.P.; two examples afford 160; two 175 and 185. The lowest of these rates of sailing may be reckoned at between six

straight line ; and if we consider that the course from Meleda requires a large circuit, and that from Malta very little, it will make the difference of distance more than 300 English miles than the distance of Malta. But, for the purpose of comparison, it may be noted that the distance from Malta to Avlona is 358 miles.

^m [There is an excellent drawing of Rhegium (Reggio) in Mr. Lear's *Southern Calabria*, 1852.—T. F.]

ⁿ Thucydid. lib. vii. c. 50.

and seven M.P. per hour, and the highest at eight—giving a
mean of seven M.P. per hour, which would be reckoned a good
one for ships of the present day.' (Appendix to *Travels in
Africa*, p. 38.)" The distance, it is added, from Rhegium to
Puteoli is about 172 miles, and that if the ship, "Castor and
Pollux," sailed seven miles an hour, the space was sailed over
in twenty-five hours. Scylax (about B.C. 350) estimated the
distance from Sardinia to Libya or Africa to be one day and
one night's sail. ("A Sardinia vero in Libyam diei noctisque est
navigatio."—*Scylacis Periplus*, cura J. F. Gail. *Parisiis*, 1826,
vol. i. p. 239.) Ptolemy mentions 1000 stadia, or 114 English
miles, as the distance a ship will sail in a day and a night.
Dr. W. Falconer, in his *Discourse on the Distance which Ships
of Antiquity usually sailed in twenty-four hours*, [translation
of *Arrian's Voyage round the Euxine Sea*. Oxford: 4to,
1805, p. 133,] came to the conclusion, in opposition to
Major Rennel, who considered thirty-seven miles to be the
average, that Ptolemy was correct in putting 1000 stadia, or
114 miles, as the average distance a ship of antiquity sailed in
a day. The ship of Adramyttium, which was to sail by the
coasts of Asia, after leaving Cæsarea, touched the next day at
Sidon, and the distance between these two places is sixty-seven
geographical or seventy-seven English miles. We know, however, the capacity of the "Castor and Pollux" to sail, and if it
did sail seven miles an hour, it would have sailed eighty-four
miles in twelve hours. On leaving Rhegium "after one day
[that] the south wind blew, they came the next day [the second]
to Puteoli," having sailed a hundred and seventy-two miles. In
what time, then, could this ship have sailed from St. Elmo to
Syracuse? An answer to this question will solve the other
question, namely, can it be inferred the vessel wintered three
months at Malta? What is the distance?

	Lat. N.		Mer. P.		Long. E.
Syracuse	37 3	..	2396	..	15 16
St. Elmo, Malta.. ..	35 54	..	2311	..	14 31
	1° 9'=69'		85		0° 45'
Diff. Long. 45' log. ..	1·653213		Course, 27° 54' sec.	10·053663	
M.P. 85' log.	1·929419		Lat. diff. 69' log...	1·838849	
Tan. 27° 54'	9·723794		78 miles	1·892512	

These 78 miles geographical or nearly 90 English miles [Becher's Tables, No. 22], was the distance which it is indisputable this particular ship could have sailed and may have sailed in thirteen hours. Can it be believed it was delayed with a perishable cargo in sailing to Syracuse during three months, if it were at Malta? The month of December at Malta is said to be a known month of fine weather [see *Meteorological Returns*]. Any long delay there could not have been involuntary. It is also not to be disregarded that the Queen Amelia Adelaide left England in October, 1838, for Malta, and remained in the island until May, 1839. It is not an island where an enforced residence for three months, on account of bad weather or the apprehension of storms during the winter months was probable in the instance of a vessel bound to Puteoli. The stormy character of a winter in the Adriatic might most certainly have detained the ship "Castor and Pollux" at Meleda. At Malta it certainly could not have wintered in what is called "St. Paul's Bay;" nor does there appear to have been any necessity for much delay in proceeding to Sicily if they had reached Malta.°—T. F.]

There was a considerable trade between Alexandria and Puteoli for other articles besides corn.

"Forte Puteolanum sinum prætervehenti, vectores nautæque de navi Alexandrina, quæ tantum quod adpulerat, candidati, coronatique, et thura libantes, fausta omina et eximias laudes congesserant: '*Per illum se vivere: per illum navigare: libertate atque fortunis per illum frui.*' Qua re admodum exhilaratus, quadragenos aureos comitibus divisit: jusque jurandum, et

---

° "At Malta, which is near two hundred miles distant, [Malta to Etna is 110 miles.—T. F.,] they perceive all the eruptions of Etna from the second region, and that island is often discovered from one-half of the elevation (10,874 feet) of the mountain."—*Travels in Sicily and Malta*, by Brydone. Catania, May 29, 1770.

"I am surprised to find that Mount Etna, though at a distance of about one hundred and ten miles, is distinctly visible from the island in clear weather. I have seen it twice from the roof of our hotel. It appeared like a white cloud on the horizon, but with a perfectly clear and distinct outline, and, with a telescope, I could distinguish the black crater and dark shadows of the sides of the mountain."—*Letters from Malta and Sicily*, by George Waring, p. 104, London, 1843. [This author says he has "not seen the observations of Dr. Falconer, but *believes* they are little more than a repetition of the arguments of Bryant"!!]

cautionem exegit a singulis, non alio datam summam, quam in emptionem Alexandrinarum mercium, absumpturos."—*Sueton. Cæsar Octavius Augustus*, ch. 98, ed. Lug. Bat. 1751, p. 334. Puteoli was the port at which the corn ships from Egypt (Alexandria) usually touched and landed their cargoes.

[Various authors, says Bryant, speak of Alexandrian ships, particularly:—

Cicero. Pro C. Rabirio Postumo Orat. ch. 14, "ductæ naves Postumi Puteolis sunt: auditæ, visæque merces fallaces quidem et fucosæ chartis et linteis et vitro dilatæ: quibus quum multæ naves refertæ fuissent, una non patuit parva atque arta."

Suetonius. In Nerone, ch. 20, "captus autem modulatis Alexandrinorum laudationibus qui de *novo commeatu* Neapolim confluxerant." Nero died A.D. 69.

Seneca. Epist. Mor. lib. x. epist. 1 [77]. "Subito hodie nobis Alexandrinæ naves adparuerunt quæ præmitti solent et nunciare secuturæ classis adventum, *Tabellarias* vocant. Gratus illarum Campaniæ adspectus est: omnis in pilis Puteolorum turba consistit et ex ipso genere velorum, Alexandrinas, quamvis in magna turba navium intellegit. Solis enim licet supparum intendere, quod in alto omnes habent naves. Nulla enim res æque adjuvat cursum quam summa pars veli: illinc maxime navis urgetur. Itaque quoties ventus increbuit majorque est quam expedit, antenna submittitur: minus habet virium flatus humili cum intravere Capreas et promontorium, ex quo

'alta procelloso speculator vertice Pallas'

ceteræ velo jubentur esse contentæ: supparum Alexandrinarum insigne (indicium) est."

Strabo, who was himself in Egypt [lib. ii. ch. 5, sec. 12, and lib. xvii. ch. 1, sec. 13], mentions the trade of Alexandrian merchants in his day to India, and the wealth derived from the general commerce of the city of Alexandria.

The trade carried on was immense. The chief commodity was corn, which was exported annually to Italy to a great amount. This freight was of such consequence that laws were enacted, under different emperors [later than the Voyage], for its regulation and despatch. Mariners, particularly, were under great restrictions, being obliged to use their utmost diligence, and were liable to capital punishment if they unnecessarily went

out of their course [Cod. lib. ii. tit. 4, "Quis fiscales," &c.]. The
magistrates and commissaries on shore suffered total confiscation
of their estates if they were convicted of mismanagement [Cod.
lib. xi. tit. 1]. And "Judices qui in portibus diœcesios suæ
onusta navigia cum prosperior flatus invitat *sub prætextu hyemis*
immorari permiserint una cum municipibus et corporatis ejusdem
loci fortunarum propriarum feriantur dispendiis. Naucleri præ-
terea pœnam deportationis excipiant si aliquid fraudis eos
admisisse fuerit revelatum." In short, no delay was allowed.
Imperial Rome, the mistress of nations and the pride of the
universe, was often in want of bread! No city suffered at times
greater scarcity; nor was there any gratuity to the people more
acceptable than a donation of corn. Augustus, when he reduced
Egypt to be a province, opened the canals of the Nile which had
been obstructed and spoiled, and exacted, by way of tribute, a
certain quantity of wheat to be annually sent to Italy. The
amount of this impost was incredibly great. If we may credit
Aurelius Victor [*Epitome de Vita et Moribus Imp.*], who lived A.D.
373, it was twenty millions of Roman modii, which, in our measure, is above one hundred and sixty thousand tons—an amazing
quantity. This was originally brought over in ships of great
burden. At the same time there were imported drugs, spices,
silks, tapestry, glass, and, in short, all the produce and merchandise of the East. Ships generally set out together, forming
a large fleet, called *Commeatus Alexandrinus*, and were consigned
to Puteoli as a harbour, drawing too much water for the river
Tiber. Before them went some light vessels, called " *Præcur-
sores et Tabellariæ*," to give notice of their approach. They were
welcome on account of their freight, and had the privilege of
entering the harbour with their *supparum*, or topsail, displayed
—an honour allowed to no other ships. Puetoli was in those
days the great emporium of Italy. Its mole is represented to
have been a wonderful structure, the foundation being formed of
a particular cement which hardened in the water. It was of
great circumference, and a large navy could ride securely within
its barrier. There was a *Pharos*, or lighthouse, near Puteoli, in
respect of which Alexandrian vessels paid toll in common with
other vessels. It is alluded to by Statius:

> " Teleboumque domos, trepidis ubi dulcia nautis
> Lumina noctivagæ tollit Pharos æmula lunæ."—*Bryant.*]

[The Narrative of the Shipwreck claims the most unbiassed and indifferent consideration of its related facts simply. It almost forbids any effort to express any particular conclusion which does not involuntarily present itself to the mind from legitimate sources of reflection and from illustrations which are so free from dispute as to be undeniable.—T. F.]

	Latitude N.		Longitude E.	
	°	′	°	′
LISSA .. ..:	43	3	16	10
MELEDA	42	47	17	8
GULF OF DRIN	41	37	19	28
DYRRACHIUM	41	18	19	26
BRINDISI	40	39	17	58
AVLONA	40	27	19	26
SASSENO ISLAND	40	29	19	14
CORCYRA	39	37	19	55
ADRAMYTTIUM	30	35	27	2
CEPHALONIA	38	28	20	33
NAPOLI DI ROMA	37	33	22	48
SPEZZIA	37	15	23	8
SYRACUSE	37	3	15	16
CERIGO	36	23	22	57
PASSARO (SICILY)	36	41	15	19
MALTA, KOURA PROM.	35	56	14	25
DITTO, ST. ELMO	35	54	14	31
CANDIA	35	21	25	8
C. CRIO	35	13	23	34
CLAUDA ISLAND	34	47	24	7
KALOS LIMNIONES	34	55	24	49

Clauda to Malta, 477 miles.
St. Elmo to Avlona, 358 miles.
Malta to Syracuse, 98 [English] miles.
Malta to Etna M. (Admiral Smyth) 110 [English] miles.
Avlona to Meleda, 151 miles.
Avlona to Syracuse, 283 miles.
Meleda to Syracuse, sailing six miles an hour, would be less than four days' sail, giving a large margin of time for deviation.

THE ACTS, CHAP. XXVII.

[Authorised Version.]

1 And when it was determined that we should sail *into* Italy, they delivered Paul and *certain* other prisoners unto one named Julius, a centurion of Augustus' band.

2 And entering into a ship of Adramyttium, *we launched*, meaning to sail by the coasts of Asia; *one* Aristarchus, a Macedonian of Thessalonica, being with us.

3 And the next *day* we touched at Sidon. And Julius *courteously entreated* Paul, and gave him liberty to go unto his friends *to refresh himself.*

4 And when we had *launched* from thence, we sailed *under* Cyprus, because the winds were contrary.

5 And when we had sailed over the sea of Cilicia and Pamphylia, we came to Myra, *a city* of Lycia.

6 And there the centurion found a ship of Alexandria sailing *into* Italy; and he put us therein.

7 And when *we* had sailed slowly many days, and scarce were come *over against* Cnidus, the wind not suffering us, we sailed under Crete, *over against* Salmone;

8 And, hardly passing it, came unto a place called The Fair Havens; nigh whereunto was the city of Lasea.

9 Now when much time was spent, and *when sailing was now dangerous, because the* fast was *now* already past, Paul admonished *them,*

THE ACTS, CHAP. XXVII.

[Revised Edition, by Dean Alford.]

1 And when it was determined that we should sail into Italy, they delivered Paul and certain other prisoners unto one named Julius, a centurion of Augustus' band.

2 And *we embarked* in a ship of Adramyttium, *which was* to sail to the coasts of Asia, *and put to sea*; Aristarchus, a Macedonian of Thessalonica, being with us.

3 And the next day we touched at Sidon. And Julius courteously entreated Paul, and gave him liberty to go unto his friends to refresh himself.

4 And *we put off* from thence, and sailed under Cyprus, because the winds were contrary.

5 And when we had sailed over the sea *which is off* Cilicia and Pamphylia, we came to Myra in Lycia.

6 And there the centurion found a ship of Alexandria sailing into Italy; and he put us therein.

7 And sailing slowly many days, and *with difficulty coming* over against Cnidus, the wind not suffering us, we sailed under Crete, over against Salmone;

8 And, *with difficulty* passing it, *came* unto a place which is called The Fair Havens; nigh whereunto was the city of Lasea.

9 Now when much time was spent, and when the voyage was now dangerous, because the fast was now already past, Paul admonished them,

THE ACTS, CHAP. XXVII.

[Revised Edition, by S. Sharpe.]

1 And when it was determined that we should sail *to* Italy, they delivered Paul, and *some* other prisoners, to a centurion, named Julius, of the Augustan band.

2 And entering a ship of Adramyttium, we launched, meaning to sail by the coasts of Asia; Aristarchus, a Macedonian of Thessalonica, being with us.

3 And Julius *treated* Paul *mildly*, and gave him liberty to go to his friends *to receive their attentions.*

, 4 And when we had *launched* from thence, we sailed under [*shelter of*] Cyprus, because the winds were contrary.

5 And when we had sailed over the sea of Cilicia and Pamphylia, we came to Myra in Lycia.

6 And there the centurion found an Alexandrian ship sailing *to* Italy, and he put us therein.

7 And when *he* had sailed slowly for several days, and were scarcely come *to* Cnidus, the wind not suffering us, we sailed under [shelter of] Crete, *by* Salmone;

8 And hardly passing it, came to a certain place called Fair Havens, nigh whereunto was the city of Lasea.

9 Now when much time was spent, and *the voyage already dangerous, because even* the Fast was already past, Paul *advised*, *saying to them;*

10 And said unto them, *Sirs*, I perceive that this voyage will be with *hurt* and much damage, not only of the lading and ship, but also of our lives.

11 *Nevertheless* the centurion believed *the master and the owner of the ship more than those things which were spoken by Paul.*

12 And because the haven was not commodious to winter in, *the more part advised to depart thence also,* if by any means they might *attain to Phenice, and there* to winter; *which attain to Phenice, and lieth toward the south west and north west.*

13 And when the south wind blew softly, supposing that they had obtained *their* purpose, loosing *thence,* they sailed close by Crete.

14 But not long after *there arose against it* a tempestuous wind, called Euroclydon.

15 And when the ship was caught, and could not bear up *into the wind, we let her drive.*

16 And running under a certain island *which is called Clauda, we had much work to come by the boat:*

17 Which when they had taken up, they used helps, undergirding the ship; and, fearing lest they should fall into the quick-*sands, strake sail,* and so were driven.

18 And we being exceedingly tossed with *a tempest, the next day they lightened the* ship;

---

10 And said unto them, "Sirs, I perceive that this voyage will be with hurt and much damage, not only of the lading and ship, but also of our lives."

11 Nevertheless the centurion believed the master of the ship, and the owner more than those things that were spoken by Paul.

12 And because the haven was not commodious to winter in, the more part advised to depart thence also, if by any means they might attain to Phenicé to winter; which is an haven of Crete, and looketh in the direction of the south-west and north-west winds.

13 And when the south wind blew softly, supposing that they had obtained their purpose, loosing thence, they sailed close by Crete.

14 But not long after *there blew from the shore* a tempestuous wind, called Euroclydon.

15 And when the ship was caught, and could not bear up *against* the wind, we let her drive.

16 And running under a certain island which is called Clauda, we had much work to come by the boat:

17 Which when they had taken up, they used helps, undergirding the ship; and, fearing lest they should fall into the quicksand, *lowered our top gear,* and so were driven.

18 And we being exceedingly tossed with the tempest, the next day they lightened the ship.

---

10 And said unto them, "Sirs, I perceive that this voyage will be with hurt and much damage, not only of the lading and ship, but also of our lives."

11 Nevertheless the centurion believed the master of the ship, and the owner more than those things that were spoken by Paul.

12 And because the haven was not commodious to winter in, the more part advised to depart thence also, if by any means they might attain to Phenice to winter; which is an haven of Crete, and looketh in the direction of the south-west and north-west winds.

13 And when the south wind blew softly, supposing that they had obtained their purpose, loosing thence, they sailed close by Crete.

14 But not long after *there blew from the shore* a tempestuous wind, called Euroclydon.

15 And when the ship was caught, and could not bear up against the wind, we let her drive.

16 And running under a certain island which is called Clauda, we had much work to come by the boat:

17 Which when they had taken up, they used helps, undergirding the ship; and, fearing lest they should fall into the quicksand, *lowered our top gear,* and so were driven.

18 And we being exceedingly tossed with the tempest, the next day they lightened the ship.

---

10 'Men, I perceive that the voyage will be *with risk* and much damage, not only of the lading and the ship, but also of our lives.'

11 *But* the centurion believed *the pilot and the owner of the ship rather than what was said by Paul.*

12 And because the haven was not commodious to winter in, *the greater number gave advice to set sail* thence also, if by any means they might *reach* Phenice, a haven of Crete, *facing away from the south-west and north-west winds,* and winter there.

13 And when the south wind blew softly, supposing that they had attained their purpose, loosening thence they sailed close by Crete.

14 But not long afterwards there beat *against it* a tempestuous wind called Euroclydon.

15 And when the ship was caught, and could not bear up *against the wind, we gave up and were driven.*

16 And running under [*shelter of*] a certain island, called Clauda, *we were scarcely able to get hold of the boat.*

17 And when they had taken it up, they used helps, undergirding the ship; and fearing lest they should fall into the [Gulf of] *Syrtis, they lowered the sail* and so were driven.

18 And as *we were* exceedingly tossed by *the tempest, the next day they began to heave overboard.*

19 And the third *d ly we* cast out with our own hands the tackling of the ship.

20 And when neither sun nor stars *in* many days appeared, and no small tempest *lay on us,* all hope that we should be saved was *then* taken away.

21 But *after* long abstinence Paul stood forth in the midst of them, and said, Sirs, ye should have hearkened unto me, and not *have loosed* from Crete, *and* to have *gained* this harm and loss.

22 And now I exhort *yon* to be of good cheer; for there shall be no loss *of any men's* life among you, but of the ship.

23 For there stood by me this night the angel of God, whose I am, and whom I serve,

24 Saying, Fear not, Paul; thou must be brought before Cæsar; and, lo, God hath given thee all them that sail with thee.

25 Wherefore, sirs, be of good cheer: for I believe God, that it shall be even as it was told me.

26 Howbeit we must be cast upon a *certain* island.

27 But when the fourteenth night was come, as we were driven *up and down in Adri,* about midnight the shipmen deemed that *they drew near to some country;*

28 And sounded, and found *it* twenty fathoms: and when they had gone a little further, they sounded again, and found *it* fifteen fathoms.

19 And the third day we cast out with our own hands *the furniture of the ship.*

20 And when neither sun nor stars *for* many days appeared, and no small tempest lay on us, all hope that we should be saved was then taken away.

21 But *when there had been* long abstinence *from food,* then Paul stood forth in the midst of them, and said, "Sirs, ye should have hearkened unto me, and not have *loosed* from Crete, and have *spared* this harm and loss.

22 "And now I exhort you to be of good cheer: for there shall be no loss *of any life* among you, but *only* of the ship.

23 "For there stood by me this night *an* angel of God, whose I am, and whom I serve,

24 "Saying, 'Fear not, Paul; thou must be brought before Cæsar: and, lo, God hath given thee all them that sail with thee.'

25 "Wherefore, sirs, be of good cheer: for I believe God, that it shall be even as it hath been told me.

26 "Howbeit we must be cast upon a *certain* island."

27 But when the fourteenth night was come, as we were driven up and down in Adria, about midnight the shipmen deemed that they drew near to some country;

28 And sounded, and found it twenty fathoms, and when they had gone a little further, they sounded again, and found it fifteen fathoms.

19 And on the third day *they* cast out with *their* own hands the tackling of the ship.

20 And when neither sun nor stars appeared *for* many days, and no small tempest *overhung, at last* all hope of our being saved was taken away.

21 But after long abstinence, then Paul stood in the midst of them, and said; 'Men, ye should have hearkened to me, and not *set sail* from Crete, to have gained this risk and damage.

22 'And now I exhort you to be of good cheer; for there will be no loss of life among you, but of the ship.

23 'For there stood by me this night an angel of *that* God, whose I am, and whom I serve, saying;

24 Fear not, Paul; thou must be brought before Cæsar; and lo, God hath given to thee all them that sail with thee.

25 'Therefore, be of good cheer, men, for I believe God, that it will be even as it was told me.

26 'But we must be cast upon *some* island.'

27 And when the fourteenth night was come, as we were driven *along in the Adriatic,* about midnight the sailors deemed *that some country drew near to them.*

28 And *they* sounded, and found twenty fathoms: and when they had gone a little further, they sounded again, and found fifteen fathoms.

29 Then fearing lest we should fall upon *rocky places*, they *threw* four anchors out of the stern, and wished for the day.

30 And as the *sailors* were *seeking* to flee out of the ship, *and* had let down the boat into the sea, under colour as though they would *carry forth* anchors out of the fore-ship,

31 Paul said to the centurion, and to the soldiers, ‘ Unless these men abide in the ship ye cannot be saved.'

32 Then the soldiers cut off the ropes of the boat, and let her fall off.

33 And while day was coming on, Paul besought them to take food, saying ; ‘ This day is the fourteenth day that ye have *been looking out* and continued fasting, having taken nothing,

34 ‘ Therefore I pray you to take food ; for this is for your *safety* ; for not a hair shall *perish* from the head of any of you.'

35 And when he had thus spoken, he took bread, and gave thanks to God in the presence of them all ; and when he had broken it, he began to eat.

36 Then were all of good cheer, and they also took *food.*

37 And we were in all in the ship two hundred and seventy-six souls.

38 And when they were *satisfied with food,* they lightened the ship, *casting out the corn* into the sea.

39 And when it was day, *they* knew not the land ; but they discovered a certain

---

29 And fearing lest we should have fallen upon rocks, they cast four anchors out of the stern, and wished for the day.

30 And as the shipmen were *seeking* to flee out of the ship, when they had let down the boat into the sea, under colour as though they would have cast anchors out of the foreship,

31 Paul said to the centurion and to the soldiers, "Except these abide in the ship, ye cannot be saved."

32 Then the soldiers cut off the ropes of the boat, and let her fall off.

33 And while the day was coming on, Paul besought them all to take food, saying, "This day is the fourteenth day that ye have tarried and continued fasting, having taken nothing,

34 "Wherefore I pray you to take some *food* ; for this is for your *health* : for there shall not an hair fall from the head of any of you."

35 And when he had thus spoken, he took bread, and gave thanks to God in the presence of them all ; and when he had broken it he began to eat.

36 Then were they all of good cheer, and they also took *food.*

37 And we were in all in the ship two hundred and seventy six souls.

38 And when they had *eaten enough,* they lightened the ship, casting out the wheat into the sea.

39 And when it was day, they knew not the land ; but they discovered a certain

---

29 Then fearing lest we should have fallen upon rocks, they *cast* four anchors out of the stern, and wished for the day.

30 And as the *shipmen* were *about to* flee out of the ship, when they had let down the boat into the sea, under colour as though they would *have cast* anchors out of the foreship,

31 Paul said to the centurion and to the soldiers, Except these abide in the ship, ye cannot be saved.

32 Then the soldiers cut off the ropes of the boat, and let her fall off.

33 And while the day was coming on, Paul besought *them* all to take meat, saying, This day is the fourteenth day that ye *have tarried* and continued fasting, having taken nothing,

34 Wherefore I pray you to take *some* meat : for this is for your *health* : for there shall not an hair *fall* from the head of any of you.

35 And when he had thus spoken, he took bread, and gave thanks to God in the presence of them all : and when he had broken it, he began to eat.

36 Then were they all of good cheer, and they also took *some meat.*

37 And we were in all in the ship two hundred threescore and sixteen souls.

38 And when they had *eaten enough,* they lightened the ship, and cast out the wheat into the sea.

39 And when it was day, *they* knew not the land : but they discovered a certain

creek with a *shore*, into the which they were minded, if it were possible, to thrust *in* the ship.

40 And when they had *taken up* the anchors, *they committed themselves unto* the sea, and loosed the rudder bands, and *hoisted up the mainsail to the wind*, and made toward *shore*.

41 And falling into a place *where two seas met*, they *ran* the ship aground; and the forepart stuck fast, and remained unmoveable, but the *hinder part* was broken with the *violence* of the waves.

42 And the soldiers' *counsel* was to kill the prisoners, lest any of them should swim out, and escape.

43 But the centurion, *willing* to save Paul, kept them from *their* purpose; and commanded that they which could swim *should cast themselves first into the sea*, and get to land:

44 And the rest, some on boards, and some on *broken pieces* of the ship. And so it came to pass, that they *escaped* all safe to land.

CHAP. XXVIII.

1 And when they were escaped, then they knew that the island was called Melita.

2 And the *barbarous people* shewed us no *little* kindness; for they kindled a fire, and received us *every one*, because of the present rain, and because of the cold.

---

creek with a *beach*, into which they were minded, if it were possible, to thrust the ship.

40 And having *cast off* the anchors, *they sent them into the sea, at the same time* loosing the bands of the rudders; *hoisting up the foresail to the breeze*, they made toward *the beach*.

41 But falling into a place *with two currents*, they ran the ship aground; and the forepart stuck fast and remained immoveable, but *the stern* was broken by the *force* of the waves.

42 And the soldiers' council was that they should kill the prisoners, lest any of them should swim out and escape.

43 But the centurion *wishing* to save Paul, kept them from the purpose; and commanded that those who could swim should *throw themselves off first*, and get to *the* land;

44 And the rest, some on *planks*, and some on *pieces* of the ship. And so it came to pass that *all came* safe to land.

CHAP. XXVIII.

1 And when they were *saved*, then they knew that the island was called Melita.

2 And the *barbarians* shewed us no *common* kindness; for they kindled a fire, and received us *all*, because of the present rain, and because of the cold.

creek with a *shore*, into the which they were minded, if it were possible, to thrust *in* the ship.

40 And when they had *taken up* the anchors, *they committed themselves unto* the sea, and loosed the rudder bands, and *hoisted up the mainsail to the wind*, and made toward *shore*.

41 And falling into a place *where two seas met*, they *ran* the ship aground; and the forepart stuck fast, and remained unmoveable, but the *hinder part* was broken with the *violence* of the waves.

42 And the soldiers' *counsel* was to kill the prisoners, lest any of them should swim out, and escape.

43 But the centurion, *willing* to save Paul, kept them from *their* purpose; and commanded that they which could swim *should cast themselves first into the sea*, and get to land:

44 And the rest, some on boards, and some on *broken pieces* of the ship. And so it came to pass, that they *escaped* all safe to land.

CHAP. XXVIII.

1 And when they were escaped, then they knew that the island was called Melita.

2 And the *barbarous people* shewed us no *little* kindness; for they kindled a fire, and received us *every one*, because of the present rain, and because of the cold.

3 And when Paul had gathered a bundle of sticks, and laid *them* on the fire, there came a viper out of the heat, and fastened on his hand.

4 And when the barbarians saw the venomous beast *hang*, on his hand, they said among themselves, No doubt this man is a murderer, whom, though he hath escaped the sea, yet *vengeance* suffereth not to live.

5 And he shook off the beast into the fire, and felt no harm.

6 *Howbeit* they looked when he should have swollen, or fallen down dead suddenly: but after they had looked a great while, and saw no harm come to him, they changed their minds, and said that he was a god.

7 In the same *quarters* were possessions of the chief man of the island, whose name was Publius: who received us, and lodged us three days courteously.

8 And it came to pass, that the father of Publius lay sick of a fever and of *a bloody flux*: to whom Paul entered in, and prayed, and laid his hands on him, and healed him.

9 So when this was done, others also, which had diseases in the island, came, and were healed:

10 Who also *honoured us with many honours*; and when *we departed*, they laded *us with such things as were necessary.*

11 And after three months we departed in a ship of Alexandria, which had wintered in the isle, whose sign was *Castor and Pollux.*

12 And *landing at* Syracuse, we tarried there three days.

---

3 And when Paul had gathered a bundle of sticks, and laid them on the fire, there came a viper out of the heat, and fastened on his hand.

4 And when the natives saw the beast *hanging* on his hand, they said among themselves, "No doubt this man is a murderer, whom, though he hath escaped the sea, yet *vengeance* suffereth not to live."

5 *So then* he shook off the beast into the fire, and felt no harm.

6 Howbeit they looked when he should have swollen, or fallen down dead suddenly: but *when* they looked a great while, and saw no harm come to him, they changed their minds, and said that he was a god.

7 In the same *quarters* were possessions of the chief man of the island, whose name was Publius; who received us, and lodged us three days courteously.

8 And it came to pass, that the father of Publius lay sick of a fever, and of a bloody flux: to whom Paul entered in, and prayed, and laid his hands on him, and healed him.

9 So when this was done, *the rest* also, which had diseases in the island, came, and were healed:

10 Who also honoured us with many honours: and when, we were departing, they laded us with such things as we needed.

11 And after three months we departed in a ship of Alexandria, which had wintered in the isle, whose sign was Castor and Pollux.

12 And landing at Syracuse, we tarried there three days.

---

3 And when Paul had gathered a bundle of sticks, and laid them on the fire, a viper came out of the heat, and fastened on his hand.

4 And when the barbarians saw the beast *hanging* from his hand, they said to one another; 'No doubt this man is a murderer, whom, though he hath escaped the sea, *Justice* hath not suffered to live.'

5 But he shook off the beast into the fire, and felt no harm.

6 *And* they looked when he should have swollen or fallen down suddenly dead; but after they had looked a good while, and saw no harm come to him, they changed and said that he was a god.

7 And in the *parts about the same place* were possessions of the chief of the island, whose name was Publius; who received us and lodged us three days courteously.

8 And it came to pass, that the father of Publius lay sick of *feers and dysentery*; to whom Paul entered in, and prayed, and laid his hands on him, and healed him.

9 So when this was done, others also who had diseases in the island, came and were healed:

10 Who also *presented us with many presents*, and laded us, *when we set sail*, with things *for our wants.*

11 And after three months we set sail in an Alexandrian ship, which had wintered in the isle, whose sign was the *Sons of Jove.*

12 And *coming to* Syracuse we tarried there three days.

13 And from thence we *fetched a compass*, and came to Rhegium: and after one day the south wind blew, and we came the next day to Puteoli:

14 Where we found brethren, and were desired to tarry with them seven days: and so we went toward Rome.

15 And from thence, when the brethren heard of us, they came to meet us as *far* as Appii forum, and The three taverns: whom when Paul saw, he thanked God, and took courage.

16 And when we came to Rome the centurion delivered the prisoners to the captain of the guard: but Paul was suffered to dwell by himself with a soldier that kept him.

13 And from thence *we made a circuit*, and came to Rhegium: and after one day, the south wind *arising*, we came *in two days* to Puteoli:

14 Where we found brethren, and were desired to tarry with them seven days: and so we went toward Rome.

15 And from thence, when the brethren heard of *our arrival*, they came to meet us as far as Appii Forum, and The Three Taverns: whom when Paul saw, he thanked God, and took courage.

16 And when we came to Rome,* Paul was suffered to dwell by himself with the soldier that kept him.

* *The words which follow here in the authorised Version, the centurion delivered the prisoners to the captain of the guard: are not found in any of the oldest MSS.*

13 And from thence *going round* we came to Rhegium; and after one day *that the* south wind blew, we came *on the second* to Puteoli;

14 Where we found brethren, and were asked to tarry with them seven days; and so we went toward Rome.

15 And from thence the brethren who had heard of us came to meet us as far as Appii Forum and the Three Taverns; whom when Paul saw, he thanked God and took courage.

16 And when we came to Rome, the centurion delivered the prisoners to the captain of the [Pretorian] *camp*, and Paul was suffered to dwell by himself with a soldier that kept him.

MALTA.

LATITUDE 35° 53′ 54″ N.   LONGITUDE 14° 30′ 30″ E.

NOVEMBER.	1864. 6 A.M.	1869. 9 A.M.	1869. WIND. MILES. ANEMOMETER.		1869.
1	W.	E.	82	63	Fine; cloudy
2	S.E.	N.E.	67	85	Gloomy
3	S.E.	E.	237	23	Fino
4	S.E.	W.	42	24	Fine
5	S.E.	N.W.	157	22	Fine
6	S.E.	N.W.	113	70	Fine
7	S.W.	W.	23	62	Fine
8	E.S.E.	W.	36	94	Fine
9	N.W.	N.E.	10	86	Fine
10	W.	N.E.	55	71	Fine
11	S.W.	N.W.	51	94	Fine
12	S.	N.W.	88	47	Fine
13	S.E.	N.E.	255	84	Fino
14	N.W.	N.E.	214	27	Fine
15	S.	N.W.	46	89	Fine
16	S.W.	N.W.	66	71	Fine
17	N.W.	N.W.	37	41	Fine
18	N.W.	N.E.	143	23	Fine
19	N.W.	E.	296	81	Showery
20	N.W.	E.	200	87	Showery
21	W.	N.W.	35	10	Fine
22	W.N.W.	S.W.	65	49	Showery
23	N.W.	N.W.	102	87	Fine
24	W.	S.E.	58	25	Fine
25	S.	S.W.	200	78	Fine
26	S.	N.W.	66	69	Fine
27	W.	N.W.	61	89	Fine
28	N.W.	N.W.	67	79	Fino
29	N.N.W.	N.W.	121	83	Fine
30	W.N.W.	N.W.	170	35	Fino

MALTA—*continued.*

December.	1861. 6 A.M.	1869. 9 A.M.	1869. Wind. Miles Anemometer.		1869.
1	N.N.E.	S.W.	58	66	Fine
2	W.	S.E.	187	06	Fine
3	W.	N.W.	139	73	Fine
4	N.E.	S.W.	41	55	Fine
5	E.	E.	133	38	Fine
6	E.N.E.	E.	213	70	Fine
7	S.W.	E.	142	28	Fine
8	S.W.	S.E.	81	46	Fine
9	W.N.W.	E.	39	67	Fine
10	W.N.W.	S.E.	56	45	Rainy
11	S.E.	N.W.	32	57	Fine
12	S.E.	S.E.	72	46	Rainy
13	S.	N.W.	147	28	Fine
14	S.	N.W.	42	08	Fine
15	S.	N.E.	57	10	Fine
16	W.S.W.	N.E.	131	73	Fine
17	W.	N.	78	16	Fine
18	S.W.	N.W.	94	15	Fine
19	S.S.W.	N.W.	111	83	Fine
20	N.N.W.	W.	79	50	Fine
21	N.W.	N.W.	55	25	Fine
22	S.W.	S.W.	109	10	Fine
23	S.W.	S.W.	82	94	Fine
24	W.	S.E.	70	51	Fine
25	S.E.	S.E.	224	37	Fine
26	S.E.	S.E.	19	56	Fine
27	S.E.	S.W.	140	19	Fine
28	S.W.	S.W.	156	01	Fine
29	S.W.	N.	60	86	Fine
30	N.	N.E.	115	21	Fine
31	W.	N.W.	119	99	Fine

I am indebted to the Committee of the Meteorological Office, and to the courteous assistance of Robert H. Scott, Esq. (Director), for the above Tables of Winds.—T. F.

I

THE FOLLOWING WORKS

WERE PUBLISHED BY

WILLIAM FALCONER, M.D., F.R.S.

1. Dissertatio Medica Inauguralis, "De Nephritide Verâ." 8vo. Edinburgh. 1766.

2. An Essay on the Bath Waters. In four parts, containing a Prefatory Introduction on the Study of Mineral Waters in general. "Neque vero inficiantur experimenta quoque esse necessaria : ne ad hæc quidem aditum fieri potuisse nisi ab aliqua ratione, contendunt."—*Celsus.* London. Printed for T. Lowndes, Fleet Street. 1770.

3. Observations on Dr. Cadogan's Dissertation on the Gout and all Chronic Diseases. 8vo, pp. 115. London. 1772.

4. An Essay on the Bath Waters. In four parts, containing a Preparatory Introduction on the Study of Mineral Waters in General :—
   - I. An account of their possible impregnations.
   - II. The most approved means to be used for the discovery of their contents.
   - III. Experiments on the Bath Waters, with an application of the foregoing rules to the discovery of their contents.
   - IV. On the effects of the Bath Waters on the human body, and the propriety of their use in Medicine, with an application of the experiments to Medicine and Pharmacy. 8vo. London. 1772. [Second Edition of No. 2.]

5. An Essay on the Bath Waters : on their External Use. In two parts,—
   - I. On Warm Bathing in General.
   - II. On the External Use of the Bath Waters. 8vo. N.D., qy. Bath. 1774.

6. Observations and Experiments on the Poison of Copper. "Neque interesso an initio pleraque explorata sint, si a consilio tamen cœperunt."—*Celsus.* 12mo, pp. 116. London. 1774.

7. An Essay on the Water commonly used in Diet at Bath. "Oportet autem neque recentiores viros in his fraudare quæ vel repererunt, vel recto secuti sunt, et tamen ea quæ apud antiquiores aliquos positi sunt, authoribus suis reddere."—*Celsus.* 12mo. Pp. 180. London. 1776.

[Dedicated to Dr. Fothergill, at whose desire the work was undertaken It contains an analysis of the various cold-water springs round Bath.]

8. Experiments and Observations. In three parts—
   - I. On the dissolvent power of water impregnated with fixible air, compared with simple water, relatively to medicinal substances.
   - II. On the dissolvent power of water impregnated with fixible air, on the Urinary Calculus.
   - III. On the antiseptic power of water impregnated with fixible air, and a comparison of several antiseptic substances with one another relative to this quality. *First Edition.* London. 1776.

9. Observations on some of the Articles of Diet and Regimen usually recommended to Valetudinarians. 12mo. London. 1778.

10. Remarks on the Influence of Climate, Situation, Nature of Country, Population, Nature of Food, and Way of Life, on the Disposition and Temper, Manners and Behaviour, Intellect, Laws, and Customs, Form of Government and Religion of Mankind. 4to, pp. 552. 1781.

[Translated and published in German.]

11. Remarks on the Knowledge of the Ancients on the Freezing of Water that has been boiled. 1782.—*Transactions of the Manchester Literary and Philosophical Society*, Vol. I. p. 261.

12. An Inquiry concerning the influence of the Scenery of a Country.— *Transactions of the Manchester Literary and Philosophical Society.* Vol. I. p. 271.

13. Thoughts on the Style and Taste of Gardening among the Ancients.— *Transactions of the Manchester Literary and Philosophical Society,* Vol. I. p. 297.

[This Essay was enlarged and published in a separate form.]

14. An Account of the late Epidemic Catarrhal Fever, commonly called the Influenza, as it appeared at Bath in the months of May and June, 1782. 8vo. London. 1782.

15. On the knowledge of the Ancients respecting Glass. 1783. *Transactions of the Manchester Literary and Philosophical Society*, Vol. II. p. 95.

16. A Medical Commentary on Fixed Air. By Matthew Dobson, M.D., F.R.S. With an Appendix, by William Falconer, M.D., F.R.S. 8vo. London. 1785.

17. Observations on the Knowledge of the Ancients respecting Electricity. —*Transactions of the Manchester Literary and Philosophical Society,* Vol. III. p. 278.

18. Observations on the Palsy. 1798.—*Memoirs of the Medical Society of London*, Vol. II.

19. On the Efficacy of the Application of Cold Water to the Extremities in a Case of obstinate Constipation of the Bowels; with Remarks thereon. 1789.—*Memoirs of the Medical Society of London*, Vol. II. p. 73.

20. A Dissertation on the Influence of the Passions on the Disorders of the Body. London. 1788.

[To this Essay was adjudged the first Fothergillian Gold Medal. Several Editions were published. Third Edition, 1796.]

21. Letter respecting the Article in the Transactions of the Manchester Society, on the knowledge of Electricity among the Ancients. 1791. —*Monthly Review*, p. 359.

22. Essay on the Preservation of the Health of Persons employed in Agriculture, and on the Cure of the Diseases incident to that way of Life. 8vo, pp. 88. Bath. 1789.

[This work was first printed in the fourth volume of the "Letters and Papers of the Bath and West of England Agricultural Society."]

23. A brief Account of the newly-discovered Water at Middle Hill, near Box, in Wiltshire. 8vo. 1789.

24. Sketch of the History of Sugar in Early Times, and through the Middle Ages.—*Transactions of the Manchester Literary and Philosophical Society*, Vol. IV. p. 291.

25. A Practical Dissertation on the Medicinal Effects of the Bath Waters. 8vo, pp. 188. Bath. 1790. *Third Edition*, with considerable additions respecting the Use of the Waters in Hip Cases. Bath. 1807.

26. Examination of two Parcels of English Rhubarb, with experiments of its comparative effects with the Foreign Rhubarb. By WILLIAM FALCONER, M.D., F.R.S., and C. H. PARRY, M.D.—*Letters and Papers of the Bath and West of England Agricultural Society*, Vol. III.

27. Results of Experiments to ascertain the Advantage of cultivating Rhubarb. *Letters and Papers of the Bath and West of England Agricultural Society*, Vol. I. p. 220.

28. An Account of the Efficacy of the Aqua Mephitica Alkalina. *Fourth Edition.* Pp. 208, *ante* No. 15. London. 1792. *Fifth Edition.* 1798.

[Translated into Italian, and published at Venice in 1790.]

29. Influenzæ Descriptio, Auctore Gulielmo Falconer, M.D., F.R.S. et C.M.S. uti nuper comparebat in urbe Bathoniæ Mense Julio, Augusto, Septembre, A.D. 1788.—*Memoirs of the Medical Society of London*, Vol. III. p. 25. 1792.

30. On the Lepra Græcorum.—*Memoirs of the Medical Society of London*, Vol. III. p. 368. 1792.

31. Case of a Man who took by mistake Two Ounces of Nitre instead of Glauber's Salts.—*Memoirs of the Medical Society of London*, Vol. III. p. 539. 1792. See Book on Medical Jurisprudence.

32. Miscellaneous Tracts and Observations relating to Natural History, selected from the principal Writers of Antiquity. 4to. Cambridge. 1793.

[" I have lately been instrumental in procuring from the Cambridge Press the publication of a work which chiefly turns upon Botanical subjects, and was drawn up by my friend Dr. Falconer, a man whose knowledge is various and profound, and whose discrimination upon all topics of literature are ready, vigorous, and comprehensive."—" I often console myself with reflecting on the sounder opinions of Sir Thomas Browne, Sydenham, Boerhaave, and Hartley, in the days that are past, and, of our own times, posterity will remember that they were adorned by the virtues as well as the talents of a Gregory, a Heberden, a Falconer, and a Percival." —*Dr. Parr's Remarks on the Statement of Dr. Combe*, pp. 71–83.

" The learned and truly pious Dr. Falconer and his excellent son."—*Will of the Rev. Dr. Parr.*]

33. An Account of the Use, Application, and Success of the Bath Waters in Rheumatic Cases. 8vo, pp. 72. London. 1795.

34. Observations respecting the Pulse, intended to point out with greater certainty the indications which it signifies, especially in Feverish Complaints.

" Nisi pulsus cujusvis hominis antea innotuerit; ex sola ejus frequentia febris certo discerni nequit."—*Burserii Inst. Med. Pract.*, Vol. I. p. 9. London. 1799.

[See Guy's Hospital Reports—Memoir on the Pulse. Dr. Bostock, in the 'Cyclopædia of Practical Medicine,' Article "Pulse," p. 656, referring to Dr. Falconer and Dr. Heberden, says, " They may justly be regarded as among the most enlightened and candid physicians of modern times."]

35. An Essay on the Plague. 8vo, pp. 72. London. 1801.
36. Letter on the Portland Powder.—*Monthly Magazine, April*, 1801.

37. An Examination of Dr. Heberden's Observations on the Increase and Decrease of different Diseases, and particularly the Plague. 8vo. Bath. 1802.

38. An Account of the Epidemical Catarrhal Fever, commonly called the Influenza, as it appeared at Bath in the winter and spring of the year 1803. Pp. 46. Bath. 1803.

[Reprinted in the 'Annals of Influenza,' p. 253; published by the Sydenham Society, London, 1852.]

39. On the Latin and Greek Names of Plants. A. Hunter's 'Georgical Essays.' Vol. V. 1803.

40. A Remonstrance, addressed to the Rev. Richard Warner, on the subject of his Fast Sermon. May 27, 1804. 8vo, pp. 52. Bath. 1804.

" Justum est bellum, quibus necessarium et pia arma, quibus nulla, nisi in armis, relinquitur spes."—*Livii lib. ix., Oratio C. Pontii.*

41. A Dissertation on the Ischias, or, the Diseases of the Hip-Joint, commonly called a Hip-Case; and on the Use of the Bath Waters as a remedy in this complaint. 8vo, pp. 55. London. 1805.

'Η δὲ νοῦσος χαλεπὴ λίην ἐστὶ καὶ χρονίη.—*Hippocrates.*

[To this Essay the Medical Society of London adjudged its Silver Medal.— *Memoirs of the Medical Society of London,* Vol. VI. p. 174.]

42. Sketch of the similarity of Ancient and Modern Opinions and Practice respecting the Morbus Cardiacus.—*Medical Memoirs,* Vol. VI. p. 1. 1805.

43. Arrian's Voyage round the Euxine Sea, translated and accompanied with a Geographical Dissertation and Maps. To which are added three Discourses:

 I. On the Trade to the East Indies by means of the Euxine Sea.

 II. On the Distance which the Ships of Antiquity usually sailed in Twenty-four Hours.

 III. On the Measure of the Olympic Stadium. By WILLIAM FALCONER, M.D., F.R.S., and the Rev. THOMAS FALCONER, M.A., formerly Fellow of Corpus Christi College. 4to, pp. 213. Oxford. 1805.

44. Dissertation on the Elysian Fields of Antiquity.—*Athenæum* (a Monthly Review), Vol. I. pp. 36, 148, 261. 1807.

45. Observations on the Words which the Centurion uttered at the Crucifixion of Our Lord. By a LAYMAN. 8vo, pp. 29. Oxford. 1808.

Οἴδαμεν ὅτι ἀληθής αὐτοῦ ἡ μαρτυρία ἐστίν.—*Evang. S. Johan.* xxi. 24.

46. Vindication of the translation of Arrian's Periplus of the Euxine Sea.— *Classical Journal,* Vol. XV. pp. 317. 1817.

47. Dissertation on St. Paul's Voyage from Cæsarea to Puteoli, on the Wind Euroclydon, and on the Apostle's Shipwreck on the Island of Melite. By a LAYMAN. 8vo, pp. 24. Oxford. 1817.

[William Falconer, M.D., F.R.S., the Author of the above works, was a son of William Falconer, Esq. (born 20th March, 1699), of the Inner Temple, Recorder of Chester, who married his second cousin, Elizabeth, sister of Randle Wilbraham, Esq., M.P., of Rode Hall, Cheshire (the grandfather of the first Lord Skelmersdale), a very eminent lawyer, D.C.L. (by diploma), and Deputy-Steward and Counsel of the University of Oxford.—Dr. F. was born at Chester, 13th February, 1744. He settled at Bath, January, 1770, and was elected physician of the Bath General

Hospital, 12th May, 1784, which office he resigned, 10th February, 1819. He died 31st August, 1824, and was buried at Weston, near Bath. His brother, Thomas Falconer, Esq., of Chester, wrote the additional Latin annotations of the edition of the *Geographiæ Strabonis*, 2 vols., folio, Oxford, 1807; and his only son, the Rev. Thomas Falconer, Fellow of Corpus Christi College, Oxford, edited the work.]

The following work was addressed to Dr. Falconer by that able and accomplished scholar, the Rev. Charles Dunster, the Author of an Edition of ' Paradise Lost,' &c. &c.

" Considerations on Milton's early reading and the *prima stamina* of his ' Paradise Lost,' together with extracts from a Poet of the Sixteenth Century (Joshua Sylvester), in a letter to William Falconer, M.D., from Charles Dunster, M.A. 8vo. London, 1800."

The Rev. Mr. Dunster was the writer of the following lines :

" Durdham, while on thy breezy down I stray
At early morn and with delight inhale
The cheering fragrance of the genial gale ;
How sweet to scent thy od'rous hawthorns gay,
Rob'd in the brightest bloom of vernal May,
Or view in yonder deep indented vale,
Mid hanging rocks and woods with whitening sail,
The tall bark frequent winds its way.

" O then to thee this artless strain I pour,
Grateful that still in numbers rude to speak,
Thy praise is mine, who pent in crowded town
Late pined the victim of disease and pain,
Till FALCONER's friendship bid me haste to seek
Health—loveliest Oread—on thy breezy down."

Half-past 7 A.M., 19th *May*, 1801.

Letter from Edmund Burke, M.P., to William Falconer, M.D.

" SIR,
" I am extremely thankful to you for letting me know to whom it is that we have been obliged for the temperate, judicious, and reasonable paper which appeared in the Bath prints some time since, and which was inclosed to me in a cover without any name. I am happy in your thinking my little endeavour in any sort worthy of co-operating towards the good purposes which your able paper was so well calculated to promote. It was very early my opinion, that even if the things which have been done in France were better done than they are, that the principles upon which the new legislators act are, in themselves, very pernicious, and cannot be adopted in any country without bringing it to shame and ruin. I am proud in finding you in the same opinion. I am perfectly sensible of my obligation to you for the pains you have taken in the various extracts which you have made for the support of our common principles, and for my instruction as well as satisfaction. It is always of great moment to every man, who in affairs of consequence is obliged to dissent with several of his contemporaries, to show that in differing from them he agrees with other persons not less respectable. The gentlemen of your faculty have long been distinguished for joining liberal erudition to professional skill. I do not know any profession which may not be aided by it as well as adorned. Your remarks show that you have gone further, and have joined to that liberal literature such a knowledge of our laws and constitution as make you valuable as a useful citizen as well as a man of letters and of medical knowledge. I see that the managers of the Revolution Society, though they broke up in the most complete distraction and mutual ill-humour, have thought proper to publish such an account, as if their madness had been quite methodical, and that they had pursued their plans of anarchy in the very best possible order. There is a vein of fraud which runs through all their proceedings.
" If your business should ever permit you to visit London, I shall be very happy if you will add to the favour of your present communication, that of per-

mitting me to cultivate a personal acquaintance with a gentleman to whom I am so highly obliged, and for whose learning and abilities, as well as for the use he makes of them, I have so sincere a respect.

"I have the honour to be, with the greatest possible attention and regard, Sir, your most obedient and faithful humble servant,

"EDM. BURKE.

"November 14, 1790.

"I beg leave to pray your acceptance of a new edition of my Pamphlet, in which you will find some particulars a little better methodised, and more clearly explained in the way of stating some facts and sentiments.

"*To William Falconer, Esq., M.D.*"]

www.ingramcontent.com/pod-product-compliance
Lightning Source LLC
Chambersburg PA
CBHW022337020726
47500CB00004B/1163